TALES OF THE

SCATTERED

Copyright © 2020 by Ty'Ron W. C. Robinson II. All rights reserved. Published

by Dark Titan Entertainment.

Also in hardcover format.

Dark Titan Universe is a branch of Dark Titan Entertainment.

First Printing 2020. Printed in the U.S.A.

ISBN: 978-1-7343300-2-1

darktitanentertainment.com

WORKS BY TY'RON W. C. ROBINSON II

BOOKS

DARK TITAN UNIVERSE SAGA

MAIN SERIES
Dark Titan Knights
The Resistance Protocol
Tales of the Scattered
Tales of the Numinous
Day of Octagon
Crossbreed (Forthcoming)
Heaven's Called (Forthcoming)

SPIN-OFFS
In A Glass of Dawn: The Casebook of Travis Vail
Maveth: Bloodsport (Forthcoming)

COLLECTED EDITIONS
Dark Titan Omnibus: Volume. 1
Dark Titan One-Shot Collection
The Swordman Collection
The Commander Norland Collection
The Chosen Son Collection
The Nano Man Collection

THE HAUNTED CITY SAGA
The Legendary Warslinger: The Haunted City I
Battle of Astolat: A Haunted City Prequel (KOBO Exclusive/Forthcoming)
Redemption of the Lost: The Haunted City II (Forthcoming)

OTHER BOOKS
Lost in Shadows: A Novel
Lost in Shadows: Remastered
Accounts of The Dead Days
The Book of The Elect
Hod
Hallow Sword: Cursed(KOBO Exclusive)
Symbolum Venatores: The Gabriel Kane Collection

ONE-SHOT STORIES
Maveth, The Death-Bringer
Mystery of the Mutant-Thing
Shade and Switchblade
Retribution of Cain
The Mythologists

TALES OF THE
SCATTERED

TY'RON W. C. ROBINSON II

CONTENTS

I

<u>LEONIDAS REBORN</u>

"I left my home of Rome to visit the country famous for its independence: The United States. Upon my entry into the country, I realized it and the neighboring lands were filled with many idols. Idols of silver, gold, wood, and stone. I assumed those idols consumed the minds of the American people and it was not so. There were others. Other idols whom they've begun to worship. These so-called 'heroes' or what others perceived as gods and titans among men. They dressed in various forms with details pertaining to ancient lands and cultures. Yet, I discover there is one among the city of Los Angeles. Now, I intend on finding this "Astonishing Voltage" to learn more about this land and their obsession with these rising figures."

Marcus took the taxi through Los Angeles, California. His first visit into the United States and all he can think of is disgust and consumerism. As the taxi drives down the streets, Marcus noticed several Voltage posters and banners laid out throughout the city and its neighborhoods. He shook his head with grief. Brushing his brown hair back and creasing his beard. The taxi driver noticed Marcus' disgust.

"What's the issue?"

"These banners I'm seeing. They really worship this guy."

"Best they worship something, right?"

"How can they choose to worship a figure who appeared from out of nowhere compared to the gods of the ancient times."

"Maybe that's what it is, sir. Gods of the past. They refused the laws of the ancients and desired what's best for today."

"And this "Voltage" figure is what's best for the modern world?"

"I can't say. I've read articles of others appearing across the country and the world. It's only a matter of time before some challenges all of them with the worship of humanity."

"May be so." Marcus said with thinking thoughts.

"You don't sound from around here."

"I'm from Rome."

"Ah. So, I take it your name is one of the Roman ones?"

"You can say. My name is Marcus. Marcus Leonidas."

"Leonidas? As in the Spartan king?"

"Yes. I am a direct descendant of Leonidas."

"How can you be sure of something like that? I thought the guy was just a character in those fancy movies."

"I've done my studies. Leonidas existed, and I am proof."

"And you've discovered your heritage in the Spartan lands?"

"Yes."

"I take it you'll put it to good use."

"That is my goal."

The taxi dropped Marcus off at the hotel where he's staying. Entering his suite, Marcus set up his gear and began his research on the Voltage. Reading articles and watching news reports of the Voltage's activities. Even going onto social media to read and watch bystanders speak about the Voltage's actions throughout Los Angeles. The reactions made Marcus angry. He closed his laptop and mediated.

"How? How can they worship a figure like this? Who makes fun of his enemies and relaxes in his stead? Maybe humanity is falling away as it was prophesied. Maybe it is time for someone to declare ruler ship over the lands to fare these heroes away."

The following day, Steve Walker leaving from college, made his way to his Grandmother's home for a visit. Approaching the door, Steve knocked as usual, even though he has a key to the place. Reaching down in his pocket, he sighed, pulling out the key as the door opened. His grandmother stood there, staring at him and glancing at the key. Steve noticed it quickly.

"I keep forgetting." Steve said with a grin.

"Yeah. Yeah."

Steve entered the home and he glanced at the TV. On the TV was the news and their discussion of the Voltage's activities in Los Angeles. Steve's grandmother sat down to watch the news and Steve sat next to her, placing his bag on the floor near the door.

"After everything he's done for the people of Los Angeles, we just

want to know how the Voltage do it?" The news reporter asked.

"Have you ever seen him? The Voltage, Steven?"

"No, Grandma." Steve said. "I've never encountered him. Would be something if I did."

"Best you don't."

"Why not? Might be a cool experience to meet one of the heroes."

"It may be. But, men like him create adversaries. Enemies with power usual greater than their own. It will only be a matter of time before someone steps up to him and challenges him."

"How can you be sure of that?"

"It's an old adage. History repeats itself. A hero is born and afterwards gives birth to a villain."

"I don't know. Maybe things could be different with this guy. I mean, he's not like the others. Someday he might stand with them in a battle or something."

"Better he remains here to protect us. The others out there have their own areas to monitor. You heard the story of some giant beast roaming through the Canadian forests?"

"I passed by it on the internet. Next to an article that said Bigfoot was seen in Retropolis killing people."

"I'm being serious." Grandma Betty said.

"I know. I'm just saying it would be better to keep watch. We never know when we'll come across one of them or their adversaries."

"Better the hero than the villain." Betty said with an assured smile.

They laugh at one another's words before Steve glanced at his phone. Seeing a message.

"What is it?"

"I have a date tonight with Emily."

"Really?"

"Yeah."

"Who set that up?"

"I did."

"What have I told you about lying to me?"

"I'm not lying." Steve said. "It's an, uh, it's a double date of sorts with Gregg and his girlfriend."

"I understand." Betty said with a smile. "Have fun. Not too much fun."

"I will." Steve said, hugging his grandmother. He grabbed his bag left the home.

Marcus remained in his hotel for hours. Meditating. Through the meditation, Marcus learned of his purpose in Los Angeles and what he was sent to do. During the mediation Marcus receive a vision from who he believes to be the Roman god Somnus, one of the gods of the Oneiri. Somnus grated Marcus a vision of a supposed future, where he overthrew the Voltage and ruled Los Angeles himself under a moniker similar to Leonidas' own title. Marcus awoke from the visitation filled with energy and increasing vigor.

"I know what I must do. I will take out the Voltage and will rule this city under changed rules. Spartan rules. I must gather what I need to begin."

Marcus bolted and left his hotel. Marcus walked throughout Los Angeles. Coming to the homeless, the gangs, and those in need. He spoke to them concerning his vision and it enticed them to potential hope for themselves within the city. Marcus gave them the choice of joining him in overthrowing the Voltage to gain their supposed rewards. Many gave in and joined Marcus. Marcus rallied his army, an army growing by numbers as Marcus was preparing the time to strike and make himself known through the city.

Later that night, Steve and Emily enter a restaurant. Emily was a young, petite woman who lets her energy do the talking for her. Which is what attracted Steve toward her. Besides their history of being in the same schools since childhood. Steve looked over to a table, seeing his friend Gregg Stykes with his girlfriend, Amanda. Gregg rubbed his head, having his haircut hours prior. His physical size was one of a quarterback football player. Steve and Emily walked over toward them, sitting at the table. Gregg shook his head. Amazed at Steve.

"What?" Steve asked.

"To see you out here with me and a girl, it's something for me to behold."

"Funny." Steve laughed.

"Tell me, Emily, how is it being with this guy? Is it strange? Kooky? Funny?"

"It's what it is. However, it works out."

"It works out, huh." Gregg shook his head. "You have one here, Steve. Maybe a keeper."

"I'm sitting right here."

"I know."

While the dinner goes on, Marcus assembled his army. An army of those who are angry and spiteful of the Voltage's successes. Many are filled with bitterness and anger of their labor proving to be unfruitful. Marcus stood with them. Rallied them up with a speech of change. The speech fired them up and they were ready to obey Marcus at every command. Marcus loved it. It reminded him of the stories written of Leonidas and he felt as if he was recreating a moment in Spartan history.

"This night, we begin the transformation of this city and the overthrowing of the Voltage!"

II

<u>CRIES OF A CONFLICT</u>

Marcus led his army into downtown Los Angeles, where he was seen by many of its residence and later the news crew captured him standing amongst his massive army. Marcus spotted them within the crowd of people. He smiled seeing his opportunity had arrived at the perfect time, pointing toward them.

"Broadcast this message I'm about to send out. Trust me, all will want to hear it."

The cameraman held up his camera, filming Marcus standing above his army and the people. The news broadcast the event live across every station. Be it on the TV, internet, or radio. Everyone in Los Angeles was capable of hearing or seeing Marcus and his army. Back at the restaurant, the TVs turned to the news and Steve saw Marcus and the army. He was applauded at the amount of people standing downtown. Gregg looked over at the TV, seeing the news and Marcus.

"Who does that guy think he is?" Gregg scoffed.

Steve grinned, but kept his attention focused at the news. Emily and Stacy didn't pay hardly any attention to the news while

Steve kept focused and Gregg continued to mock Marcus and the people.

Marcus nodded toward his army and waved at the people in the crowd.

"Citizens of Los Angeles, I am Marcus Leonidas. I have been told both by historians and researchers that I am a direct descendant of the Spartan King. But, as of my most recent visit to this city I've discovered something more about my heritage. Something that many of your will disregard completely. Yet, the few that I have assembled have already believed and are hoping for a better future. A future that I will provide for them."

"And what is this future?" A bystander asked.

"Why it is a future where the poor are no longer the poor. Where everyone will be treated as equals. No discrimination. No hatred. No envy. Just a love for all and a love for the new world."

"And you will lead this new world?"

"Absolutely. Not because I'm a descendant of Leonidas. No, no. I am much more than a descendant. I am Leonidas himself. Reincarnated into this modern world."

The crowd became confused. Hearing Marcus' words and yet they did not and could not fathom the idea of Marcus being Leonidas reincarnated. The army which Marcus assembled believed and they believed fiercely. Marcus held his hand up to silence the audience. As they silenced, he smiled.

"Let me explain so that you all might understand." He said. "The reason of my arrival to your city is not only because of the people and the cultures. It is more so due to the rise of these figures across your country. Coming from out of nowhere to protect those who can't protect themselves. Figures that resemble the gods of the ancient past. Yet, there is one of them amongst you. Residing in our city. The one called The Astonishing Voltage."

The crowd understood Marcus' words of reason to a degree. Yet, they all cheered when the name of the Voltage was spoken. Their cheers angered Marcus as he stomped, letting out a loud banging sound to follow. The crowd silenced and was slowly entering a sense of fear. A fear Marcus knew they would have at his presence.

"As of this moment, I am calling out the Voltage to come and face me in a battle. Therefore, we may see who is truly fit to protect those of this city."

Steve thought and made his decision. He stood up from the table with Gregg and Emily looking at him with confusion.

"Where are you going?" Gregg said. "You see what's happening downtown."

"Yeah. That's why I must leave."

"What for?"

"Trust me, it's important."

Emily followed Steve toward the exit. She stopped him from leaving and he turned back toward her. Seeing the confusion in her face. He wished he could reveal the details he knows, but is aware of the consequences that may follow after such actions are revealed.

"I have to go." Steve said, hugging Emily. "Next time."

"Next time." Emily said slowly.

Steve exited and ran toward a secure location. Finding a spot within an alleyway, Steve opened his backpack, revealing a suit. The Voltage suit. Detailed in its yellow color with blue details layered across with lightning bolts on the arms and legs. On the chest was the emblem of the Voltage. The letter 'V' made with striking bolts. His eyes coated in red. Steve donned the suit. Becoming The Astonishing Voltage. He struck out from the alleyway in a bolt of lightning. Through the air, the Voltage moved. His body transparent made of electricity and moving at quick speed.

Marcus awaited the Voltage's arrival and egged the crowd on further with his plans for control and eliminating the heroes from the world. The news continued their broadcasting. Gregg, Stacy, and Emily remained at the restaurant watching the broadcast.

"Where is your city's hero?" Marcus gloated. "Why hasn't your protector shown up to confront me?"

From the sky bolted down Voltage. He stood face to face with Marcus. Marcus relished in his confrontation. The crowd cheered the Voltage's arrival as Marcus' army prepared themselves for any possible outcome. Marcus measured the Voltage. Nodding and grinning at the same time and yet, in between.

"Who are you and what do you want?" Voltage asked.

"I wanted to see you. See if you would truly show up to protect these people. Yet, here you are. A man of your integrity."

"You challenged me to a battle. Why?"

"To see if this city is worthy of you."

"You believe you could do a better job at this than me?"

"Yes. I certainly can and I will once I take you out."

Marcus extended his hand outward and from his army came a staff. Marcus caught the staff in mid-air. The staff was gold and resembled the javelin of Ancient Sparta. Voltage was impressed at Marcus's skill.

"You're amazed." Marcus said.

"In a way. Yes."

"Shall we begin?" Marcus asked, twirling the staff.

"Ready when you are."

Marcus lunged toward Voltage, who vibrated his body into a non-physical form. Allowing Marcus to flow through him. Marcus paused, turning around seeing the Voltage in physical form unharmed.

"How?"

"It's one of the tricks I learned."

Voltage fired small lightning bolts toward Marcus. He deflected the bolts with the twirling of the staff, knocking them into the night sky. The sound of a small crackle could be heard above them. Marcus smiled facing Voltage.

"Try something else."

"Sure thing."

Voltage spread out his hand, facing Marcus and out of them blasted a scattering of electricity. The electricity jolted Marcus while he made the attempt of wiping the air clean of the electricity. Voltage watched as Marcus wiped and twirled the staff to rid of the floating lighting cloud.

"You might have to try something else." Voltage said sarcastically. "Maybe, a few more twirls will do. Maybe."

Marcus, unable to eliminate the cloud turned toward his army. Pointing the staff toward Voltage, the army jumped and attacked Voltage. They surrounded him. Kicking and stomping him into the ground. Marcus on the other hand had other plans. He left the area with a few of his army. The crowd scattered to get away from the growing battle. The police arrived with Sheriff Jack Martin at the lead. Voltage spotted Martin and kicked up from the ground, taking out those of Marcus's army.

"Good to have you hear." Voltage said.

"That should be my line not yours."

"Yeah, but it's the other way this time."

Voltage, Martin, and the police take charge against Marcus's army. Marcus himself made his way toward the Mayor's office where he's taken the Mayor hostage and rid City Hall of its people. Marcus stat at the Mayor's desk and nodded.

"This is where it begins. My world begins here and now."

Marcus slammed the staff into the floor. Outside on the building fell banners. Red and gold banners across nearly every building in downtown Los Angeles. Voltage and the police settled with the army started to notice the falling banners.

"What is happening?" Voltage asked.

"Looks like an invasion if you ask me." Martin replied. "A strange one at that."

The banners continued to fall, featuring a emblem that was once a symbol for the ancient Spartans. At City Hall, Marcus walked out, decked in a uniform fit for a Spartan King. He carried with him the staff and a helmet. Marcus stopped to look at the falling banners across the city. He smiled. Relishing in all he saw.

He placed the helmet over his head. A Spartan helmet fit for a warrior.

"Every man in this city will become my soldiers. Every woman will become my wives and concubines. The children will be mine to raise. I am no longer Marcus Leonidas of Rome. I shall be called King Marc of New Sparta."

King Marc stood with his army, dressed in Spartan armor themselves, cheering and yelling in celebration of what has transpired.

WELCOME TO NEW SPARTA

King Marc released his army across the city. Spreading out amongst the districts. Banners of New Sparta continued to fall upon the buildings as the visible sky was filled with the red banners. While his army went into the city, Marc made his own destination for the Staples Center. Gathering a small army that he could, he ransacked the sports arena, eliminating all who would not agree to his terms. Marc walked into the area and stood at the center. He relished his presence within the arena.

"This will be the place for those able to fight. To join the ranks of my army and for those who desire entertainment."

The city had transformed into immediate chaos with Marc's Spartan-clad army invading the neighborhoods and spots where most of the civilians were occupied. Voltage, seeing it unfold thought of his grandmother. Voltage took off and went to his grandmother's home, not before changing out of the suit and into his common clothing. Entering her home, he found her sitting at the TV, witnessing all that was transpiring in the city.

"Grandma, you have to get out of the city."

"And where will I go?"

"I have a friend who lives outside of the city limits. You can sit tight there while all this is taking place."

"What of you? Will you be coming along with me?"

"Emily will be. I won't."

"And why is that? Do you want to die at this man's hand? Or his army's?"

"No. Grandma, I feel like I can help these people in a way."

"You're not one of these heroes, Steven. You're just a young man with so much potential. Besides, you don't need another one of those accidents to occur again."

"Yet, that accident helped me realize my true potential. I can at least try to help people escape from this harm."

Betty nodded. She stood, grabbing a suitcase with clothes and her purse. She left the home with Steve. While packing the car, Emily and Gregg ran up toward them, startling them for a second. Gregg catching his breath, pointing toward downtown.

"You see what's happening out there?"

"I've seen it with my own eyes."

"What are we going to do?" Emily asked. "I'm trying to figure things out."

"Hey, where's Stacy?"

"She went home." Gregg said. "She didn't want to hear what we had to say. Quite a stubborn girl."

"You picked her."

"Where are we going to go?" Emily asked, hearing the screams in the distance.

"You'll be going with Grandma to the outskirts."

"What's out there?"

"I have a friend who lives there. You'll remain there until all of this is cleared through."

"What about you?"

"I'm going to do my best to help these people get out. As many as possible."

"You might need my help." Gregg said with a smile.

"Maybe." Steve chuckled.

"You know I can help, man."

"Yes. I know."

"By the way, where is the Voltage in all of this?" Gregg wondered. "I haven't seen him at all out here."

"He's probably deep in the downtown area." Steve said. "Or getting people out of the city. Either one."

"Yeah." Gregg replied. "You're probably right. I can help him."

"Do your best and stay safe."

"I will." Gregg said, running toward the downtown area.

Betty and Emily enter the vehicle, preparing to leave. Betty turned to Steve.

"Who is this friend of yours?"

"His name is Rax Thompson."

"Why haven't I heard of him?"

"It's a complicated issue, Grandma." Steve replied. "Secret Service type of stuff."

"And where are we to go exactly?"

Steve reached into his pocket, pulling out a map of the city and its outskirts. On the map is a marked location of Rax's residence. Steve handed the map to Emily who gazed at it and the marked spot. Betty looked at the map and nodded.

"Just follow this and it will lead you to his residence. He already knows you're on the way."

"Hopefully I can find a way to beat the traffic."

"Take the shortcut route. It's best to avoid the crowds."

"Are you sure you'll be safe?" Betty asked with certainty.

"I'll be fine, Grandma. Trust me."

They drive off from the home, leaving Steve standing in the street. He nodded, turning his attention toward the city.

"Back at it again." He said, changing back into the Voltage suit.

He charged his way through the air toward City Hall. Upon approaching it, he noticed there were more banners across the city and in front of City Hall stood a statue. The statue was of Leonidas I. The City Hall sign no longer said Los Angeles replaced with New Sparta.

"He's gone all out with this Sparta feel."

Voltage took a notice there were less and less police officers roaming the street and more of Marc's army growing by the numbers. Voltage couldn't find Sheriff Martin on the streets and it concerned him. Nevertheless, Voltage made his stop at City Hall to confront Marc. Voltage arrived at City Hall, finding it surrounded by several of Marc's armored soldiers.

"Guess I have to take these guys out."

Voltage moved at a quick pace and his body becoming nonphysical once again, knocking out the soldiers one by one with electrifying punches to the faces. Voltage morphed into his physical form as the soldiers fell to the floor. He nodded taking looks at the downed soldiers.

"That was easier than I expected."

Voltage barged into the Mayor's office and inside was no one. Voltage circled the office and it ached him not having confronted King Marc. On the desk Voltage saw details and files containing the interior of the Staples Center and other landmarks across the city.

Across the city, Marc's army rallied up all the men, women, and children they could gather. Bringing them to the Staples Center. They entered the area and inside was a major change of renovation. The interior was transformed into a gladiatorial battlefield. It looked like a mixture between modern stadiums and the ancient Roman Colosseum.

Marc stood in the middle of the arena while the soldiers escorted the citizens into the arena. They sat in fear and were kept watched by nearby soldiers. Marc raised his arms, gathering their attention toward the floor. Slamming the staff into the sandy ground.

"Ladies and gentlemen. I am aware you haven't become yet used to the recent changes of your city. Trust me, sooner or later, you will understand why Los Angeles has become New Sparta. This arena fits perfectly for a place of entertainment. Tonight, there will be fights for your amusement."

From the field entrance is thrown out Sheriff Martin. His clothing torn from the recent fights and scuffles he had to endure.

Martin is tired and worn out. His eyes can't bare the bright lights beaming down above and he can hear the screams of those in attendance. A terrible scream for help. Martin stood up to face Marc. Marc scoffed at him, gazing at his worn-out clothing.

"A Spartan does not dress in the apparel you have decided to wear."

"I'm not Spartan." Martin said. "I'm an American and this is my home you've invaded."

"Your home is gone, Sheriff of the Force. It's mine now."

Marc turned his focus back toward the crowd. He raised the staff, pointing it at Martin. Martin stood still and kept his eyes on the staff. Marc smiled.

"Who's ready for the fight of the night?!"

From the surrounding entry points, more of Marc's soldiers arrive and they're coming for Martin. Martin only has his fists and legs to defend himself since his firearm was taken from him by Marc during the street scuffles. Marc noticed Martin's movements when reaching for his gun.

"You want a weapon to defend yourself. Understandable."

Marc tossed Martin a wooden stick. Martin started at the stick. Rough in feel and heavy in wielding. He looked upon Marc who stood with his arms out wide and a big smile on his face as the soldiers inched closer.

"Do the best you can. For the people."

Martin battled the warriors with the stick. Getting a few hits in before being taken down due to his tiredness. The warriors gazed up at Marc, sitting on a pedestal looking down at them. He extended his arm and gave them thumbs down. The warrior went to a swipe of the sword and across the field a lightning bolt knocked the sword from the warrior's hand. They turned and in a blink of an eye, the Voltage intervened, taking them out with lighting. The crowd cheered seeing the Voltage staring at Marc. Marc doesn't take the cheering kindly as he jumped down from the pedestal to face Voltage.

"I've been wanting to see you."

"Here I am." Voltage said. "Again."

"You interrupt my moment of entertainment like this is your place."

"Hey, I do live in this city."

"You need to be taught a pure lesson."

"What kind of lesson do you have in mind? A history lesson?"

"It pertains to history. Which states those such as yourselves only have a short time in this world before you're taken out."

"Taken out by whom or what?"

"By men like me."

Marc swiped the staff toward Voltage and he dodged the attack. Voltage yelled for Martin to exit and he ran off, leaving Voltage and Marc on the battlefield. The crowd cheered seeing them come to blows. The soldiers stood their ground to watch the incoming battle. The warriors were left on the ground, their bodies jerking from electrical circuits. They circled one another, ready to strike.

"Guess this is what they want. A king against a outsider."

"More like an outsider against a hero."

IV

FOR GLORY'S SAKE, WAR

Betty and Emily arrived at Rax Thompson's home in the outskirts of the city. His home is a small one. Not as big as a neighborhood home or a small cabin. Yet, it fit in between the two structures in appearance and size.

"A secure place." Betty said.

"How can you be sure?"

"Look at it. No one would ever dare to bother someone in a place like this. It's too secluded."

They approached the door and Betty knocked. The door had opened and standing there was a young man. Very young which caused Betty and Emily to take a moment of pause. The young man's presence threw them off. Dressed in green buttoned shirt with black slacks and shoes. Wearing a pair of glasses and with wavy, yet scruffy black hair.

"We're looking for a Mr. Rax Thompson." Betty said. "Is he here?"

"He's me, ma'am."

"Wait. What?" Emily jolted. "You're Steve's friend?"

"Steve Walker? Yeah."

"I'm Steve's grandmother. He sent us here for protection."

"You've come to the right place."

Rax allowed them into his home and when they walked in, they were surrounded by dozens of electrical equipment from desktops to laptops to monitors to tables of miniature devices. Emily believed she was walking into a shack and Betty thought Rax was some sort of hoarder. Rax closed the door.

"No disrespect, but, how can you be Rax?" Betty asked.

"It's my age isn't it."

"It is."

"People always judge someone by their youth. Always."

"How old are you exactly?"

"Fourteen. I'll be fifteen in a matter of months."

"And Steve sent us here for protection." Emily jumped. "By a fourteen-year old?"

"It's no disrespect." Betty declared. "I never assume someone of your age would be capable of a place like this and all that's sitting in here."

"It's from my line of work."

"Work?" Emily said. "You have a job too?"

"Yeah. I work for an organization. Which is why all this equipment is sitting here. Part of the job."

"And what is this organization, if I may ask"

"One that deals in secrecy. Pertaining to these rising figures across the world."

"You deal with them?" Emily asked. "Those heroic ones out there?"

"Not all of them. Just a few."

"Like which ones?"

"Uh. There's one I met up in Canada. Another nearby Chicago and one strange one that comes and goes around Detroit. But, I haven't met every single one."

Rax settled them into his home. In the home, he showed them several rooms. Rooms that can't even be seen from the outside by the seclusion of the home's structure. Betty knew for sure the home wasn't a standard one and Emily was just coming to the realization that things aren't as simple as she once believed.

"You can stay here for as long as you need or require."

"Will you be able to contact Steve from here?" Betty asked.

"I can."

Rax left Betty and Emily to their rooms while he returned to his study, looking at a map. The map was of Los Angeles and on it were blinking lights. Lights signaling trouble. Another map sat beside it, one of the world and it was marked with stamps detailing events across the world pertaining to the rising figures.

Marc ran toward Voltage with the staff in front, Voltage grabbed the staff with his reflexes and tossed Marc across the field. Marc slid on the field and stopped himself mid-slide. He paused and thought, staring at Voltage with anger in his eyes. Voltage tossed Marc his staff and he grabbed it swiftly, standing up on his feet.

"Go another round?" Voltage asked sarcastically.

"This isn't some game you're playing."

"You're sure about that?"

Marc slammed the staff into the ground, causing a small

tremor which knocked Voltage on his knees. He gazed around his surroundings and from there, Voltage raised his left arm, shooting out a lightning bolt, to which he grabbed and allowed the bolt to carry him into the air as he held himself against the wall. Marc was astounded by Voltage's feats.

"How could you do that?"

"Do what?"

"All of which you've done?"

"Long story. Electrical accident and so on. Might be boring for a lot of people. But, it's given me this gift or curse. I haven't decided what to call it yet."

"This isn't fair."

"Fair to you or to me?"

"Who do you assume I'm speaking to? I don't have such gifts as you possess. Yet, I am from Leonidas. Therefore, I will claim your abilities and use them for my own purposes."

"Not sure how you're going to go about doing that?"

"I'll find a way. After I've finished you off in front of your city and its people."

In the crowd, more of Marc's guards bolt through. Walking with them is Gregg in handcuffs. Voltage spotted him moving through the crowd. He turned to Marc and turned to Gregg. Unsure of what he should do next. He sighed to himself as Marc continued to taunt him of his abilities.

"Let's continue this fight." Marc said. "Come on!"

Voltage bolted himself toward Marc and Marc swiped the staff, connecting it to Voltage's back causing him to fall to the ground. Voltage rolled, and Marc followed him. Laughing and mocking.

"Something's tipped you off." Marc gestured.

Marc stood over Voltage as he returned to his senses. Marc kicked Voltage in the ribs and started stomping him in the chest. The crowd continued to gasp at the sight of the Voltage laying on the ground while the soldiers cheered on their leader. Marc relished the moments he had stomping the Voltage. Feeling the might of overpowering him and proving him to be a failure to the city is what Marc wanted and now he had it in his grasp.

"You're just another one of the failures." Marc said, keeling down. "Remember that."

"Remember why?"

"Don't play coy with me. I can tell by the sound of your voice and your quickening clouded mind you're just a young man trying to help the weak and helpless and that is our downfall. Because soon, they will betray you and you'll see things from my end."

"Are you sure?"

"I am."

"That's good to know." Voltage kicked up, knocking the staff from Marc's hand.

"You bastard."

"No talking. Just fighting."

Voltage swiped Marc to the ground and stood over him, pummeling him with his fists. Each shot moved quicker and quicker until his fist couldn't be seen by the naked eye. The soldiers jumped down from the seats, running toward Voltage. Voltage watched and he bolted himself around them in a circle. All the soldiers could see was a circular lightning bolts moving around them and after the bolt cleared, the soldiers were down, jolting from a shock. Gregg jumped up in the audience, cheering on the Voltage's feats. Voltage looked up toward him and nodded. Voltage pressed his foot on Marc's chest and faced the crowd.

"The city is yours one again. Take it and be proud."

The civilians cheered the Voltage's victory and he took in their cheering. Gregg cheered even greater jumping up and down in the stands with his hands cuffed.

The police gathered and took each of the soldiers to prison. Including Marc.

The citizens took back their city and celebrated the following day. They cheered the Voltage's name through the streets. Sheriff Martin found the Voltage near the outside of the building.

"You mind if I have a word with you?"

"No problem."

"I want to thank you for what you've done. Helping us and the people of this city is certainly a great thing."

"I was only doing what I came to do."

"I know. Now, I can't convince others of the force to believe in you and what you can do. All I am saying is, I know you'll be there when the time calls for it."

Martin extended his hand toward him. Voltage looked and gave Martin a nod, shaking his hand. Martin nodded and walked. While walking away, the wind blew past him quickly with a sparking sound to follow. He smirked and continued walking. Gregg ran over toward the spot, gazing around. He turned seeing

Martin walking away and ran toward him.

"I missed him, didn't I?"

"Yeah, son." Martin said. "You did."

Betty and Emily returned to the city where Steve came to assist them. They enter Betty's home and settled in. Emily hugged Steve again as did his grandmother.

"We didn't know Rax was just fourteen." Betty said.

"I didn't want to tell you the first time."

"Why not, Steven?"

"Because you wouldn't have gone over there if I did. You wouldn't have decided to remain in the city."

"Good thing you didn't tell me."

The front door knocked, and Gregg entered. He ran toward his friend cheering and yelling. Emily moved out of the way, backing away from Steve and Gregg. Preferably Gregg.

"He's happy about something." Emily said.

"You won't believe what happened, man."

"What happened?"

"I saw the Voltage take down that Spartan guy and his soldiers in the arena. It was incredible."

"Incredible? Really?"

"Well, I would say it was astonishing."

"That makes some sense. Did you manage to get a photo or something?"

"Nah. I missed him right afterwards. I was close though."

"Maybe next time."

"Next time will be the moment."

In prison, Marc was escorted to a cell. The cell sat near the end of the hall and they opened the door for Marc to enter. Closing the door and walking away, Marc sat on the bed and remained silent. Within the room with him were others. Three men. They approached Marc, standing over him. Marc looked up at the men and he could sense their demeanor.

"How did you manage to get in here?" Marc asked.

"We have our own stories to tell."

"Stories, huh." Marc gestured. "What kind of stories?"

"Stories that feature the Voltage. We know what you done out there. You've made a name for yourself in this area. King Marc, huh."

"That is who I am and who I will always be."

"Great. Because we have a plan to get out of this place and deliver some payback on this city's great hero. Are you in?"

Marc thought and only showed a grin.

Steve returned to his apartment later in the day, focusing on his college work. While working, a knock came from the door. Steve stood up from his messy desk and answered the door. Standing there facing him was a young woman. The woman wasn't Emily. Her dark brown hair was distinct enough to tell her and Emily apart. Yet, they both had similar physical features.

"Ava." Steve said. "What are you doing here?"

"I just wanted to see how you were."

"Oh." Steve nodded. "Ok."

BIONIC RAGE: UNITED NATIONS

I

BROKEN PARTIES

Dameon Mason sat in his home. Mediating. Angry. Angry at what he's become and who he must now face. Facing the world in his current circumstance is a tension for fear amongst humanity. Yet, with all the others roaming the earth, Mason's mind is clear, and he knows he can't remain hidden forever. Mason heard knocking coming from the front door. He stood up and answered. His friend, Brad Carpenter stood before him. He nodded as Mason allowed him to enter.

"Figured I would show up." Carpenter said, removing his brown coat.

"I appreciate your concern." Mason replied. "But, why have you come now?"

"To see if you're truly ready to return to civilization."

Mason nodded. His answer was unseemly, yet, he knew he had to return. In a manner unclear to even himself. He looked at his bionic arms and legs. He touched the reactor device on his chest. Brad watched him and saw a bit of sadness within Mason's eyes. Part of his humanity is gone. Taken from him without warning.

"I can only guess how hard it must be. Your arms and legs being replaced by technology. Even with that thing in your chest powering them."

"It runs a system through my nervous system. Bio-nanotechnology. Keeps my arms and legs on par with my body."

"Don't you have some sort of scientist who can assist you with changes if necessary?"

"Not now. Which is why I must return to the open world. Find someone who can work with bio-nanotech. To help me understand what I have to live with for the rest of my days."

Carpenter nodded. He exhaled and shook his head. Rubbing his arms slightly while Mason prepared himself to leave the home. Grabbing a large brown leather coat to cover his bionic limbs from the public. Mason buttoned the coat to also cover the reactor.

"You know in time, the public will witness your newfound body."

"Let it be when the time is accurate. Now is not the appropriate time to show off what I have become."

"Understood."

"Speaking of things, where is Claire?"

"She's held up with her business nowadays. Keeps her focused. You know, more goal-oriented."

"I see." Mason nodded.

Mason walked toward the door and Carpenter followed him. As the door opened and Mason took one step out, he gazed around the surroundings. Only seeing buildings and home. Few people walking on about. He felt slightly comfortable at the scenery.

"Where are you heading?"

"Just going for a causal walk. Clear my head of my worries."

Mason exited the home. He and Carpenter went their separate ways. Mason walked for miles in the Detroit neighborhoods. Never getting tired and he knew why. His legs didn't have to deal with the weariness of the flesh. He both liked it and hated it. It gave him a sense of empowerment and a loss of what it is to be human.

While walking and mediating, screams echoed from a nearby alleyway. Mason stopped and listened. The screaming of a woman. Young. Preferably in her mid-20s. Mason could figure it out just by the sound of the scream. He moved with haste toward the alley and discovered the woman surrounded by two men. Appearing to be dressed as one of the homeless. They stood over her laughing. Each unbuckle their belts in the process to have their way with the young woman. Two thoughts entered Mason's mind. Should he help the woman or go on his way. Mason fought within his mind and made a choice without hesitation.

"Leave the woman be." Mason said.

"Keep walking." One man gestured.

"Only when you've left her alone."

The two men scoffed at Mason, turning toward him and measuring him. They nodded to one another. Believing they could take down Mason. Their confidence was high and nothing of the ordinary could bring them down or instill in them a sense of fear. They were keen on doing what they desired. They stood side by side facing Mason. Pride emitted from their being. They were young men and Mason felt sorry for them.

"Or what?"

"You won't like what comes next."

"I think we will. Once we've dealt with you, we're going to have some fun with this woman. She's young and she's fresh."

"I didn't want it to come to this." Mason said, removing his coat.

"The hell?!" One man yelled seeing Mason's bionic limbs and the reactor.

One reached into his side and started firing at Mason. He deflected the bullets with his bionic hands while approaching them. He grabbed the gun from his hand and squeezed it into rubble. One of the men stood back, yelling at his partner to find a way to take him down. The man tried punching and kicking Mason and it didn't faze him. He ran as he friend attempted to go ahead and rape the woman. Mason stood over him and picked him up from his belt and slammed him into the brick walls. The man fell to the ground, where Mason rolled him over on his back, discovering he had killed him. The man's partner took off and ran. The young woman backed up as she stood.

"Don't be afraid." Mason said. "I only came to help."

"I thank you." The woman replied. "But, you're freaking me out. What are you?"

"Something else." Mason said softly.

The woman ran and Mason turned back to leave the alley.

But, there was a man standing in his presence. The man was dressed sharp in a black suit and white tie. He wore a black fur trench coat. Mason put his coat on to cover himself, but the man had already seen enough.

"Who are you?" Mason asked.

"Spencer Vargas. I'm a native to this city and I just so happen to see you save that pretty girl from my guys."

"They worked for you?"

"Yes. For good reasons."

"And that gives them the right to rape a woman?"

"No. it gave me the opportunity to meet you."

"I'm not understanding."

"I've heard about you. Your accident and how you survived. Now, my people, if we were to have survived something like that, they'll kill us in the emergency room. Label it as an accident. But you. One of the privileged. You received special treatment and was given a new life."

"A life I didn't choose to have."

"You have it anyway. Which is why I have something to offer you."

"What might it be?"

"A job offering."

"You want me to work for you?" Mason gestured. "I don't see how that would happen."

"You have a gift, or I should say gifts." Spencer clapped. "What you have, can change this world for the better. Starting with this city."

"I'm not using these limbs to suit your own wills."

"Come on. Think about it. You've heard all about those others out there. Protecting the cities and whatnot. Detroit has no rising hero to protect it. Only the criminals control this place and I intend to be at the top of that list."

"You want to protect the people of this city?"

"In my own way. The ways we have now are useless. Only with a strict rule and a firm hand can we make things change for the better."

"How come you can't accomplish it by yourself or with your men? Why do you ask of me?"

"Because of what you have!"

"I'm sure you can find someone else with my limbs who can do a better job."

"I can't."

"Then, good luck being a hero."

Mason walked away. Spencer nodded with a strict look as he turned around and walked out of the alleyway, looking at one of his men. Seeing his dead body lying on the cold ground. He shook his head.

The following day, a visitor came to Mason's home. Mason had opened the door and standing there was Kenari Clark. Mason was aware of the Canadian businessman of Cherub Enterprises.

"Mr. Dameon Mason." Kenari said. "I take it you know who I am."

"I know who you are." Mason replied, looking at Kenari's attire. Dress formal, yet, not in a suit. "You dress differently than most businessmen in this country.”

“I have a different culture than most.”

“Why are you here, visiting me?”

“Colonel Evan Nader of T.I.T.A.N. has chosen you to be a possible candidate for his team. To combat a major threat that’s coming toward this world.”

Mason had shaken his head and nodded with a grim look. Thinking. Kenari stared at him. Studying his body language and motions. Taking notice to Mason’s bionic limbs and the reactor. Kenari senses Mason didn’t like what he had heard. Mason giggled quietly to himself.

“I can sense you find this very amusing.” Kenari insisted.

“You can say that. Because, I’m already aware of Nathan Hawke being involved in all of this.”

“He is involved. That is true. But, what does that have to deal with myself meeting you?”

Mason stepped out from the door. Showing Kenari his full body. The transformation it has taken. The bionic limbs glowing with the reactor. The green glow shined across the ground and the outer walls of the home.

“So, you’re the one who survived the explosion during the war. The one who had the secret procedure.”

“You’ve read up on true history I can see. Hawke is responsible for my current condition. I don’t take it lightly to hear he aids the Nano Man over in Newark. Sorry, but tell Colonel Nader I decline his offer. If I desire to help, it will be on my own terms and not on the sidelines with Hawke.”

Kenari nodded. “I respect your decision. It’s been a pleasure speaking with you."

Kenari had walked away. Mason watched him leave his premises and shut the door of his home.

II

<u>OPENINGS AND CLOSINGS</u>

Mason took himself another walk through the neighborhoods to clear his head. After being visited by Kenari, Mason felt his bionic limbs trembling and the reactor spiked in its use. Mason figured it was best to go on another walk to calm the bio-tech. While walking, he was found again by Spencer Vargas with two of his bodyguards.

"You again."

"I figured you would show up around this spot." Spencer mentioned. "I can see my prediction came to pass."

"I thought I already gave you an answer when I walked away."

"I know. I assumed you did that just to leave behind the mess you made."

"I did what I had to do."

"And it suited you well for the day. Not so much for the days after."

"What have you done?"

"I cleaned up your mess. Had my guy's body burned and

searching for the other. Don't worry, I already have a guy doing the searching. He's good at it. Almost like a lion hunting its prey."

"Why don't you keep him to do the other job?"

"He's not fit for other purposes. Besides, the opening I have is only suitable to men such as yourself. Military trained. Skilled in the art of war. A combatant full of techniques capable of winning a battle."

"The war ended some time ago." Mason mentioned. "Why is it still such a burden upon your mind?"

"The war proved something to me. I didn't have the opportunity to be involved as much as I desired. The war showed me things can change within a heartbeat and I aspire to make that change come to Detroit. To show all of its citizens this city can be seen for the better in this country and not a lesser state of a place."

"I understand you drive for this cause. But, I only live here to keep myself in the peace of my own mind. I don't care what happens to this city, this country, or the world. I've lost all that I possible could have and I won't desire to achieve something else in this life. It's all temporary."

"Yes, it is." Spencer said. "Just like living is only temporary. You never know when you may be sniffed out of existence."

Mason's watch began to tick. He looked at his left wrist, seeing the time within his arm. Spencer was astounded. He smiled staring at Mason's arm. The bionic features and the glow it emitted.

"What you have could change billions. Could help billions live a better life in a better world."

"Maybe. But, I don't intend on helping. I intend on staying to myself. Where I belong."

Mason covered his arm.

"If you'll excuse me, Mr. Vargas. I have a meeting to attend to."

"A meeting? You?"

"It concerns me deeply." Mason said. "Don't follow me."

Mason turned and walked away. Spencer hated the sight of Mason leaving his presence. Spencer returned to his SUV. Inside, Spencer pulled out his cell phone and dialed a number.

"Sorry to disturb you, I have another job for you once you're finished with the first."

Dameon stood in front of an office building. The word "lawyer" caught him off guard as he slowly took steps toward the entrance. Inside, he found himself being looked at by those in suits and ties. They stared at Mason for his dress and his demeanor. His wavy and scruffy hair. When he walked, a loud stump followed giving the people more reason to take an interest in him.

Walking further down the hall, Mason spotted Brad, who signaled him toward the open office. Mason approached Brad as they entered the office.

"Figured you would receive the notice." Brad said.

"I did. Stuff getting used to all of this. The change."

"It'll take some time. But, he wanted to meet you."

Mason looked up toward the desk and sitting in front of him is Nathan Armstrong. A lawyer, one who had learned the story of

Mason's accident. Nathan's office is decorated with mostly light brown colors and textures. The office had the appearance of an old-time room mixed with a 60s feel. Nathan wore a great suit and black tie. His appearance was calm and confident. A handsome man some in the building have referred to him as. Nathan extended his hand toward Mason.

"I'm not here to cause you any distress." Nathan said. "I'm just a lawyer who wants to help you."

Mason shook his hand in haste. Nathan nodded.

"Would you shut the door for us, Mr. Carpenter."

Brad closed the door and sat next to Mason while Nathan prepared himself to speak toward them both. Mason doesn't want to be in the office and Brad himself preferred to be somewhere else at the time.

"I won't keep either of you long. Trust me."

"That's a start." Mason said.

"Fair. I'm here to give you support for your change."

"What kind of support did you have in mind?"

"Well, for starters, some insurance should get you cleared up. Just in case any medical emergencies come your way through the means of your bio-nanotechnology."

"No need." Mason said. "I can control it myself."

"Are you certain of that?"

"I live with it every day since the accident. I think I can hold my own when it comes to it."

"That's a start." Nathan nodded. "What else may interest you for protection?"

"I can protect myself."

"I believe that. But, what happens if you're out there and you injure someone by accident. Let alone kill somebody. How would you fare against the police and the Federal Law?"

"I dealt with similar causes during the war. It wasn't an issue to me then. Why should it be an issue now? Because I'm less of a human than I was before?"

"That's not what I was getting at."

"You know it's true."

"Only you can be the one to answer such a question. I'm here to help you. This appointment today is designed to give you some comfort."

"Comfort?"

"Yes. During times like these, men such as yourselves are prone to violence when unnecessary. You flip out like a switch when things turn a slip."

"Mr. Armstrong." Brad said. "Just for clarity, Dameon doesn't have PTSD."

"Are you sure of that, Mr. Carpenter? Because from what I have already learned from him, he has more than PTSD. He's near gone mad."

"I am not mad."

"Listen to your words. You've basically given up living. You prefer to stay to yourself only to get away from society. You don't desire comfort or even love."

Dameon removed his coat, showing Nathan his entire body. All the bionic limbs and the reactor in his chest. Nathan took a step back and covered his mouth. Brad held his head down. Dameon's expression revealed all Nathan needed to see. He was a man of sorrows. Pain, guilt, and anger flowed through him greatly.

"How do I deserve those things when I'm... I'm like this?" Tell me?"

"I can't tell you, Dameon. Only you can tell yourself what you truly need. Not I."

"So, why am I here?" Mason stood up from the seat and left the office.

"I'm sorry about all of this." Brad said toward Nathan.

"It's fine. I learned all I needed to know about your friend. He needs help. Whether he wants to believe it or not. Otherwise, he won't end up on the bright side of life."

Mason walked with haste to exit the building and doing so, his limbs were revealed to those inside. They froze in their places and gasps came out of their mouths. Mason noticed their staring and bolted out of the exit. Brad followed him outside into the snowy weather.

"Let me give you a ride home at least."

"I can get there myself!" Mason yelled.

Dameon stopped in his tracks and from his arms and legs blasted the sound of rockets. Fire emitted from them, catching Brad off his guard. Within a quick second, Mason was in the air. Flying off. Brad watched his friend fly off. His coat flowing through the air.

"He can do that?"

Brad reached into his pocket for his cell phone. He called a friend. Someone he can speak with concerning Mason. He waited for them to pick up the other end.

"Claire." Brad said. "Look, we need to meet. It's about Dameon."

In another part of Detroit, the homeless man who escaped the alleyway was hiding inside an abandoned home. He sat on the cold ground in front of a fire made from paper and little wood. He had been there for at least two days in hiding. Sitting in the empty living room, he heard creaking sounds coming within and through the home. Knowing he wasn't making any movement, he looked around the corners to see if it was another homeless person or an animal.

"Who's there?" He asked.

From the corner came a man. Asian descent. Wearing all black. Covered from his neck to his feet. His eyes were focused on the man and he gazed once toward the fire.

"You know why I've come."

"Look, please tell Spencer that I wasn't in my right mind. It was only an accident."

"Spencer doesn't pay me to give him words from those he wants dead."

The man in black quickly rushed toward him, putting out the fire and slashing his throat with a kitana. The homeless man fell into the ashes of the flame as the man in black left the home. Exiting, he was confronted by Spencer.

"The job is complete." The man said.

"I thank you, Chiang Tojo, for your great assist in this cause."

"My pleasure." Tojo said. "And the second offer you had for

me?"

"Dameon Mason. The man who survived the war. He's been given a new life. One with bionic limbs. I want you to kill him. Remove the bionic technology from his body and deliver them to me."

"And what do I receive after this Mason is dead?"

"A great reward. One far richer than pearls and rubies."

Tojo nodded with a grin. "You'll have your bionic technology soon enough."

III

BUSINESS IS BUSINESS

Dameon was in his home with Brad and Claire. Claire, a close friend to the two a with an on-and-off relationship with Dameon spoke to him concerning his meeting with Nathan Armstrong. Dameon was certain he was right to do what he felt. He believed himself to be right in the matter. Claire and Brad disagreed with Dameon's choice.

"What's the real concern?" Mason asked.

"We're worried about what you might do." Claire said. "There's no telling if whatever is flowing through your body is messing with your mind."

"I'm not drugged. This technology keeps me focused. It keeps me alive."

"We know." Brad said. "Just let us help you in some manner. In some form."

Claire brushed back her long blonde hair while she sat back in the chair facing Mason. Brad nodded and Dameon took the seconds to think.

"If you truly want to help me, then help me stop Spencer Vargas."

"Who's he?" Claire wondered. "We're never heard of someone with that name."

"He's in the city. His men are running ramped under his orders. He wants to make Detroit a better place. But, his actions have proven otherwise."

"Have you seen his actions?" Brad asked. "Were they positive or negative in nature?"

"Two of his men attempted to rape a young girl. A girl in her twenties. They were relishing in the moment until I stepped in and stopped them. Spencer witnessed what I did, and he was impressed. He tried to recruit me into his vision of the future."

"You turned him down?"

"I wasn't going to align with a man who lets his own people do such heinous acts."

"I can understand." Brad said. "Anyhow, where do we find him? I also have ot ask do we get the police involved?"

"Rather you not." Dameon pointed. "Leave this to ourselves."

"The police can help us far more than random sightings." Claire said. "Why not bring them into this?"

"You said you wanted to help me. This is what I mean by helping me."

Claire shook her head and Brad laid back. Dameon only stared at them both with intensity. They nodded slowly.

"Fair enough." Brad said. "Never thought I would be doing something like this."

"It's no different than a standard mission."

"Lucky for you, I was there for the first half."

"You held your own out there." Dameon said. "I'm sure you'll do it again."

"Only when the situation calls for it."

Claire stood up from her seat and walked toward the door. Dameon followed her before she had a chance to open the door.

"Where are you going?"

"I'm going to have a word with that lawyer you met earlier. See if I can get some extra help in all of this."

"Are you sure about having him know?" Brad asked. "Like seriously?"

"He's a lawyer. Besides, he's already met you. What else could possibly go wrong?"

Claire stepped out of the door.

"I'll contact you when I have something to share."

"Thank you, Claire." Dameon said with a smile. "You're always helpful."

"When needed." Claire grinned.

Chiang Tojo locked himself in a dark room. The room is covered with military files and Intel records. The listings on the records include Dameon and his actions in service. Tojo studied every inch of the records to learn about Dameon. He later came to the knowledge of learning the accident which gave Dameon his bionic limbs. Tojo was impressed by the research. Studying the detail photos of the procedure. Seeing Mason laying down on the operating table without his arms and lower legs. The amount of blood in the photo gave Tojo comfort. The man can still bleed. Tojo sat back in his chair, tossing the file onto the desk.

"How will I lure you out?"

Tojo stood up from the desk and walked toward the window. Removing the curtains and looking out at the city of Detroit. Snow continued to cover the land. Tojo thought and he thought. Returning to the desk, he glanced at a map of the city and nodded with a grin.

"I have an idea."

Spencer sat down in an undisclosed location. His surroundings covered with bodyguards. Armed and loaded. Their faces covered with masks. Some dressed in suits. Others in cargo gear. Spencer spoke on the phone. Laughing and jeering.

"It's only a matter of time." Spencer said laughing. "I'll have everything settled soon."

Spencer nodded, listening to the speaker on the other end of the phone. He was loving what he was hearing. The large grin on his face. He nodded.

"I have a man already on the job. He'll deliver the bionic technology very soon. I am confident he won't make a mistake. He's done a great job once. I'm certain he will repeat his actions. They don't refer to him as the Assassin just to have a standard codename."

Spencer hung up the call. Placing the phone on his desk. He laid back in his chair with his hands together and a smile on his face. Giggling under his breath.

Claire had entered the law firm, walking down the hallway to meet Nathan. She came to his door as he was stepping out. The two bumped into each other like a door hitting against the wall.

"I'm sorry, ma'am."

"Don't be. It's my mistake. I'm here to see you anyway."

"Who are you?"

"Claire Lyons. I'm friends with Dameon Mason and Brad Carpenter."

"Oh. And I suppose they sent you here to speak with me?"

"No. I chose to come here to speak with you. Figured I could do a better job than the two of them."

"I understand. Come on in and have a seat."

Claire entered with Nathan behind her, shutting the door. The two sat down at the desk.

"What do you have to tell me about Dameon Mason that I already haven't learned by his actions?"

"He's a good man. Deep down. It's just he's still coming to grips with his current condition."

"And do you know how to calm him during this time of his?"

"I think I do. But, I'm not sure it would help him in anyway."

"How so?"

"Part of me believes the experiment they did to him altered his mind. He's not the same man I once knew."

"You believe he's changed. changed so much he isn't even the same guy who survived the accident?"

"In some way, I believe so."

"Mason showed me his bionic features in a fit of anger. I don't understand how it must be to have lost limbs of your body from such an accident."

"I have to ask. Will you help me concerning legal matters? If they come up in the future?"

Nathan looked at Claire and saw the sincerely within her. Her trust for Dameon and their relationship flowed through Claire's words as she spoke about him.

"You have my word." Nathan nodded. "Just give me a little time."

"How much time?"

"Enough for me to process all of this. Especially dealing with him if his temper manages to peak again."

"There is one more thing I have o ask of you."

"Go ahead and tell."

"Dameon was certain there is a man in the city. Spencer Vargas. Ever heard of him before?"

Nathan thought.

"I've come across that name before. During a court case concerning a troubled mother and her son. The father was killed in a gang war. Spencer Vargas came in and assisted the family. They said he was a good man to them. Gave them a home, food, and clothes."

"Dameon believes he's the opposite of those things."

"How does he know this?"

"He said he came across him few days ago. Said Spencer proposed to him a job to be at his side as he begins to make a change to the city."

"What might this change be? If you know?"

"I don't know. You'll have to ask Dameon about all of it.

From what I know, Dameon turned down he offer. Said he found two of Spencer's men attempted to rape a young woman. Dameon stopped them before they committed the act."

"Jesus." Nathan muttered. "Did the men survive the encounter with Dameon?"

"I'm not sure. He didn't say."

"And this is the reason why I'm here. Just in case Spencer would make the attempt to press charges on Dameon or the police confronted him, I would be there at his side to stand guard."

"Thank you." Claire nodded.

"It's why I'm here, Ms. Lyons."

Claire stood up and shook Nathan's hand and left his office.

Dameon and Brad were sitting in the Detroit Public Library. Brad gathered several books containing military works. Dameon stat in one place. Covered in his coat. his arms and legs unseen.

"Maybe these have some information we can use."

"We know enough. There's no need to gather more of the same techniques we already know."

"I still have much to learn. You have to figure out how'll you do."

"These arms will handle themselves. There's firepower in them."

"Gunfire power?"

"It has an alteration in them at the wrist. Pistol, rifle, or machine gun focused. I'm still learning how to use them."

"Then, where are the bullets? In your arms?"

"They move through the bicep to my wrist. Like an assembly line."

"And do you manually have to reload or does the nano-tech create the rounds from your blood or something like that?"

"Manual reloads." Dameon laughed. "I haven't reach that peak yet."

"I was certain."

Screams began to echo though the library floor. Growing louder by the seconds, Dameon and Brad stood up, seeing Tojo walking with his kitana in hand. Brad stared. Dameon could only wonder as the civilians in the library began to panic and run. A crowd of people between Dameon and Tojo.

"I believe I've found the man I'm searching for." Tojo said.

"You could've called me out in a field somewhere. Not enter a library to start a fight."

"I could have. But, there would be no one around to watch you die and your tech ripped from you."

"Who is this guy?" Brad asked.

"He's one of Spencer's men."

"I am not. I was hired by Spencer to take you out and to deliver your bionic limbs. That is all."

Tojo raised the kitana. "I believe this is the moment where you say goodbye to your friend."

"I'm not going anywhere." Brad said. "You fight him, you fight me."

"Agreed." Tojo smiled.

Tojo rushed toward Dameon with the kitana. Swiping it in the air. Dameon used his arms to block the attacks. The kitana tearing through the sleeves of Dameon's coat. revealing his arms with the glowing emitting from the tears. Brad rammed Tojo in his chest and he kicked Brad to the floor. Tojo was solely focused on Dameon and the two continued their doge and weave fight. Dameon grabbed the kitana and elbowed Tojo in the nose before tossing the kitana across the room.

"Face me like a man."

"If you wish."

Tojo moved his hands back and forth. Using several kung-fu techniques and fighting styles against Dameon. He was uncertain of the attacks as they manage to get several hits to Dameon's face. Dameon fell back, taking a breath. Brad grabbed Tojo by his arm and was slammed. Tojo stomped on Brad's chest and Dameon ran over, tacking him to the floor. Dameon raised up his fist and went to punch Tojo. He moved his head as the fist crashed into the floor, cracking the ground.

"Impressive." Tojo said, looking at Mason's bionic arm.

"There's more." Dameon stared.

Dameon raised up his right arm. It began to click. The clicking continued and it flowed through his arm and reach the wrist. Brad looked and noticed. He listened to the sound closely.

"Shit."

From Dameon's wrist flew out rounds of bullets similar to the firing of a machine gun toward Tojo. He ran and hid behind a wall while Dameon fired. He yelled loudly and walked near Tojo firing the rounds. Tojo looked over toward a desk, seeing his kitana and ran. Rolling on the ground to grab the sword. He made the decision to leave the scene, feeling it was best and Dameon ceased his firing. The floor was covered in bullets as police arrived. They entered and saw Dameon and the bullets. Brad stood up and pointed toward the outside.

"The man you're looking for just left."

55

IV

<u>UNIFIED AGREEMENT</u>

Mason and Brad left the library after being questioned by the police. They saw Dameon's bionic limbs and were terrified. They've only heard about him and the accident, but to see him for themselves, they felt both frightened and sadden. More authorities went out into Detroit to find Tojo.

"What now?" Brad asked.

"We find Vargas and Tojo. End all of this today."

"I have a possible idea."

"What is it?"

"You can go after Tojo. Let me find Vargas."

"Are you sure of doing this? Taking this part in your own plan?"

"Only way to be certain is to do it." Brad laughed. "Plus, it lowers the workload on yourself."

Dameon nodded with a grin. "I get your point. Find Claire. I have a sense she's already on Vargas' trail."

"That's what I was going to mention."

Brad left mason at his home. Dameon walked down into his basement. The basement was covered with military fear. From bulletproof vests to range weaponry. Guns of every variety hanged from the steel wall. Dameon approached the wall and stared at the guns.

Tojo ran into the office of Vargas, startling the bodyguards. His pace was quick and smooth. No emotion on his face. But, tiredness had revealed itself and Vargas could see it.

"What happened out there?"

"Ran into Mason and his friend. I wasn't aware his arms were capable of firing rounds."

"His arms turned into guns?"

"No. there are guns loaded in his arms. I watched him load them up. They fired like a machine gun. I had to hide myself. Otherwise I wouldn't be speaking to you right now."

"I like this." Vargas smiled.

"I don't. he's more than what you told me ahead of this deal."

"Because I only assumed he was a man with bionic limbs. Nothing more. But now, you come in here and tell me his arms can fire machine gun rounds. I wonder what else they can do. Probably can blast a missile too. The possibilities."

"I'm only interested in killing him and deliver what I promised. As you should be."

"Don't worry yourself over this inconvenient turn of events. I have already spoken with those who seek Mason's bionic tech and they are astonished to have learned about it."

"Who are these others? Will they interfere with my part in this deal?"

"Your part is as important as theirs. They're counting on you just as I am."

"If you say. I will only give one warning. Mason's not a calm indicial. He's a walking bionic rage."

"Intriguing. I have to learn more."

Vargas approached the door with two of his bodyguards. Grabbing his coat as the door opened for him.

"What am I to do next?" Tojo wondered. "I need to know if you have a possible lead to lure Mason in."

"There's one. Look for his friend. The one you saw in the library. Or else. Find the woman. Claire Lyons. She's close with Mason. Very close."

"How can you be so sure of this?"

"My contacts know a lot. It's their specialty."

Claire and Nathan drove through Detroit. Taking with them a map of Vargas' possible places of visitation. From banks to landmarks to restaurants. Each of them have a small hint toward Vargas. None of them have enough evidence to find him. The driving irritated Claire. Never having been used to searching for someone within the criminal element. Nathan understood her behavior and could only nod.

"One of these places must have a trail."

"Give it some time, Claire. One will pop its way in our faces."

"I hope so. I wonder what Dameon and Brad are up to."

"Probably the same thing we're doing right now. Searching for Spencer Vargas."

They moved down the road and standing by the signal light on the sidewalk is Tojo. He glanced at the car, seeing Claire and Nathan. He reached into his pocket and pulled out a photo. It was dirty and cut. On the photo was Claire and Mason. Before his accident. Mason was dressed in his military uniform and Claire was hugging him. They were smiling. Tojo nodded and put the photo back in his pocket. He moved to follow them.

Brad had entered the same neighborhood where Dameon had stopped the two men from attempting rape. He walked around the neighborhood and stopped at the spot. Seeing only a cleaner area. He went in and searched. Looking for any evidence. He found none. Turning around to return to his business, he was confronted by two armed men. They grabbed him. Brad fought back against them, but their strength overpowered Brad's punches and kicks. They knocked him out with the butt of their rifle and dragged him into a black SUV.

Brad had awoken to find himself in a large concrete room. He could see Detroit out of the large windows around him. He glanced over, seeing Claire and Nathan. Both tied up to the chairs. Brad himself was also tied down.

"Where are we?" Brad asked.

"I don't know. Why are you even here?"

"I was searching for a way to track down Vargas."

"You too, huh?" Nathan mentioned." Should've done this a

different way."

"You're in here for the same reason?" Brad asked Claire.

"We drove around to different places where Vargas operated. We came across one building that was used as a delivery center for food and we were ambushed by Spencer's men and some Asian guy with a sword. They put bags over our heads and brought us here. Wherever this is."

Brad scoped the place as best as he could. Looking at the walls and the surroundings. The smell of gunpowder caught his attention quickly.

"I think we're in a manufacturing building."

"What gives you that idea?" Nathan asked.

"Gunpowder. Don't you smell it?"

"I do." A voice from within the shadows.

Walking out toward them was Vargas. His armed men surrounded the three and Tojo stepped out beside Vargas.

"The hell did you bring us here for?" Brad asked.

"I figured after what happened at the library, it would be best to lure Mason to us. The only way to do so what to capture two of the people he's most close to."

"You did a good job apparently." Nathan mentioned.

Vargas looked at Nathan with confusion. He pointed toward his men, gesturing toward Nathan and they didn't say a word. He nodded and gazed his sights toward Tojo, who stood boldly and calm.

"Who is this man?"

"He was with Claire when we captured them. It appears he's a lawyer."

"No shit? This is good. Hell, this is gold."

"I don't know how you'll get Dameon to come here."

"I have a way and it's very simple. Call him."

Vargas dialed a number on his cell phone. Mason prepared himself in the basement. Geared up. He heard the phone ringing and he answered it with both a calm and haste.

"Who is this?"

"Spencer Vargas. Remember me."

"How did you get this number?"

"Don't concern yourself about it. You can change it after we're done doing business."

"I have no business with you. I turned down your offer."

"That was to be my bodyguard. I have another proposition for you."

"I don't want your offers."

"You'll want this one."

Vargas moved the phone over to Brad, Claire, and Nathan.

"Don't fall for it, Dameon!" Brad yelled before being hit in the ahead by one of the bodyguards."

"What have you done with them?"

"You find out. Follow the pathways I've laid out for you. Come and you'll see your friends again and you'll make a better decision."

"You better pray I don't make it. Otherwise, that whole place will covered in your blood and the blood of those standing with you."

"Come and let's find out. You have an hour." Vargas said, hanging up the call.

Dameon slammed the phone and took a moment to breathe. His anger tampered up and the green glow in his arms and legs came brighter. The reactor starting to ring a low tone. He set up his gear. Loading his arms with rounds. He went to grab his coat and paused, looking over to the closet and finding a vest. The vest was a dark brown and leather.

"It'll do." Mason said, grabbing the vest from the hanger.

Vargas walked around the three, taunting them. Tojo wanted to kill them and Vargas stopped him.

"Give it time. He'll be here soon."

"You heard what he said." Brad mentioned. "He's going to slaughter all of you."

"He will die before he makes a move!" Tojo yelled. "I will make sure you're watching when I cut your friend's head off his shoulders and I rip apart his bionic limbs."

"I'll be a witness to your death when he kills you." Claire said. "That way only one of us will be making it out of here alive."

Tojo rushed toward Claire. Their eyes locked on one another. Vargas walked up and placed his hand on Tojo's shoulder. Pulling him back. Tojo stepped back and Claire only kept her glare steady.

"She's a strong one." Vargas said. "It's best you leave her be."

"I will deal with her after Mason is dead."

"Maybe."

"I'm not understanding why you managed to keep me here." Nathan said. "I'm just a lawyer."

"Who's trying to help Mason by searching for me!" Vargas said. "Why else would you be here?"

"I was doing Mr. Mason a favor. His friend a favor."

"Look where it has brought you. Tied up to a chair, set up to die from a gunshot to the head."

"You're going to kill us, then?"

"Once Mason is dead and his bionic tech is ripped from him. Yeah."

Dameon stood outside of a large building. An old one. Older than most of downtown Detroit. Reaching into his vest pocket, he glanced at a tracker map on a device he carried. Like a Smartphone in appearance. Given to him by Brad for use when necessary. He traced the call to within the old building. The scent of gunpowder caught him and it grabbed him.

"Just like the fields." He said while moving swiftly toward the building.

Vargas began moving his men around the building. The building held four floors in total. The armed men each went to different floors to keep guard from Mason's entrance.

"They won't stop him." Brad said. "You're going to get all of you killed."

"Shut up." Vargas said. "Do that for me. At least that."

"But, he's right." Nathan added. "You're going to have your men and yourself killed from Mason's growing rage."

"His bionic rage is none of your concerns." Tojo said. "I will calm him by giving him a quick death."

On the first floor were five armed men. Moving from every possible entry into the building. Everything was quiet until Mason entered without hesitation. Busting down the wooden door. Blasting rounds of bullets at the armed men. He rammed into one of them, smashing their face in with his fists. Another tried to attack him from behind, only to have the bullet ricochet into his forehead. The following three-armed men each took their shot at Mason. He moved quickly, killing one with a blast of the rounds. The second, he grabbed and through against the wall and stomping his chest in. the last one, Mason shot in the knees. The armed man removed his mask, screaming in pain as Mason walked slowly behind him.

"Please, don't!" The man yelled.

"Too bad." Mason replied, shooting the man in the back of the head.

The gunshots could be heard on the fourth floor and Vargas smiled. Tojo grabbed his kitana quickly. Gripping the handle. Vargas signaled to the other armed men to go and find Mason. They moved out.

"He's here, huh?" Brad said. "Great."

"Don't get your hopes up." Vargas said. "He's still got two more floors to go before he reaches us."

"And he will." Claire added. "Just you wait."

The second floor, Mason did the same. Taking out the seven men that were guarding the floor. Killing them with the rounds and smashing their heads into the concrete floor. One of the men Mason had killed with his own armored vest. Twisting it as it stabbed into his own chest.

The third floor, Mason was surrounded by ten armed men. They moved stealthy around to confuse him. In between Mason and the men was a small room with glass windows. A small office area. The office furniture remained. Dusty and still. Mason felt it was best to fire rounds through the windows to startle the men and it did. Afterwards, he went out and fired shots to their legs, blowing their knees out. As each man screamed, Mason killed them with either another shot to the head or a ramming punch to the face. One man jumped Mason from behind, grabbing him and trying to hold his arms down. Mason fought back, raising his arms and breaking one of the man's arms. Mason held him by the throat and crushed his neck. He dropped his body and went up the stairs to the fourth floor. Reaching the floor, he saw Brad, Claire, and Nathan tied to the chairs and Vargas standing in the middle of them. Smiling.

"You asked for this."

"You did, I'm afraid." Vargas said.

"Above you!" Claire yelled.

Mason turned around and Tojo dropped onto him. Mason felt to the floor as Tojo swiped the kitana around Mason. Cutting his chest and his neck. Dameon stood up and grabbed Tojo, shoving him across the floor. The two stood up, staring each other down.

"This won't end like the library." Tojo said.

"I'm aware."

"Only one of us will live to see tomorrow."

"It'll be me." Dameon grinned. "I already know."

They rammed into each other. The kitana clashing against the bionic arms. Tojo used his martial arts to combat Mason. Dameon stayed with the punches and kicks. His bionic limbs would carry their heavy weight when colliding with Tojo's body. He was impressed at the amount of pain Tojo could take. Such as himself in similarity. Blood of both men was spilled on the floor. Mason punched Tojo and busted his nose. He grinned, kicking Mason in his abdomen, causing him to fall. Tojo ran and stomped on the reactor. The reactor glowed, and Mason yelled. He was feeling pain.

"Excellent." Vargas said with an astounding voice.

"Come on, old friend!" Brad yelled. "Get up!"

Tojo raised the kitana and impaled it into Mason's left shoulder. He went to grab the kitana and Tojo kicked his hand away. Enjoying the moment. Even more than Vargas, who was salivating over the scene.

"Are you ready to die, Bionic Rage?"

"Not yet." Mason said. "Just not yet."

Mason raised his right arm toward Tojo's face. The wrist had clicked and Tojo turned.

"You are."

From his wrist blasted a miniature missile. Blowing Tojo's head completely off and the remains splattered across the room. His brain matter was on the floor and the wall. The blood had covered Mason's chest and parts of his face.

"Shit." Vargas said.

Mason stood up, looking down at Tojo's dead body. He moved and released the three from the chairs and snatched Vargas. He held him by the throat. Ready at any moment to kill him and he wanted to.

"Wait, Mason." Nathan said. "Let's take him to the

authorities.”

“Why?”

“They can deal with him and if you come up, I can assist you. As I promised your friend, Claire.”

Mason looked back at Claire, who smiled. He gazed over to Nathan and nodded. Dropping Vargas onto the floor. Spencer coughed as Mason stepped away from him.

“You think this is all set and done?” Vargas asked. “It’s not. I’m not the only one who has entered your life this way, Dameon. There are others. Many who seek what you have, and they will do anything to achieve it.”

“Who are they?” Mason asked.

“They’re on their way to the city. You’ll learn of them soon.”

Mason stopped in his tracks. Listening to the words Vargas had spoken out.

“One thing.”

Mason turned around and punched Vargas, knocking him out. Mason choice to leave as Nathan contacted the police. The police had arrived and arrested Vargas. Forensics and detectives arrived to look at the kills delivered by Mason. They only knew Vargas’ men were killed by something strong. They related the kills to a military slaughter.

Days later, the city of Detroit had learned about Mason through a ongoing codename, Bionic Rage. Spencer Vargas was placed in prison and received a letter from the United Nations to discuss the bionic technology Mason possesses. Another man by the name of Chris Stanton had entered Detroit. Unknown to most of the authorities. He's a mercenary and the only thing he carried with him was a photo of Mason. Claire and Brad worked with Nathan to get Dameon clear of any possible legal charges.

Mason remained at his homestead and on the news, he saw the city of Retropolis being attacked. On the TV, he recognized a few of the figures.

"That's what he meant."

He stood up and prepared himself as Brad entered the home. Brad saw his friend geared up.

"What's going on now?"

"I'm going to help a fellow friend."

Mason pointed toward the TV and Brad saw what was happening.

"Is that what I think it is?"

"It is. They need me to help and I'm going."

"Aren't you concerned about what the public may assume?"

"Not anymore." Mason said. "They have a name for me now. They know I'm around."

He had himself prepared.

"I'll be back soon enough."

"I know."

Mason left the home and made his way toward Retropolis to assist The Resistance.

TERROR: BEHOLD, AGENCY X

I

HIDDEN PAST

John Terror made his return to Chicago, Illinois after assisting The Swordman in his mission against J and Sir Onyx. Terror's first order of business finding the secret laboratory that resides within Chicago. The laboratory itself is a secret place, hidden from amongst the masses that reside within the city or those who live outside of its limits.

Terror found his way to the laboratory. Deserted from the outside. Terror parked his motorcycle, walking towards the laboratory doors. The building resembled a factory for shipping transportation machinery. Terror found himself a way in from the sides doors. The front doors were locked as he suspected. Terror walked inside. the lights of the interior off and the surroundings silent. Terror scoffed at his surrounding, searching for the light switch. He found it and set the lights on. The surroundings brightened, and terror could see what was truly sitting within the factory-molded building. Terror saw surgery tables, medical tools laying atop desks and trays. There were even IV poles set against the nearby wall.

"What is this place used for?" Terror asked.

As he walked through, he found more medical materials and machinery. He was already aware the place wasn't used as a factory as it appears to the outside. Terror had found the laboratory. Terror searched for an office, pertaining to have clues sitting on the office desk. Searching around the laboratory, Terror found the office and kicked in the door. He approached the wooden desk and sitting on it were files. A plethora of them in alphabetical order. Terror picked up the files, disregarding their ordered setting and opened them. He read the documents. Each of the files were given a name. names after their patients. Terror read them.

"Ariana Cerra, Marth Randolph, Jr., Lois Frost, Scott Branagh, Daniel Summers, Danny Blake, and Isabel Dotson."

Terror shrugged his shoulders as he dropped the files onto the desk. He continued to look around to find something that could trace him to the laboratory's owner and their business. Terror glanced at the board and written on the board was "Agency X". Terror glanced more so.

"Agency X?" He questioned.

Terror decided to read what was written on the board and out in the open area of the laboratory, the sound of the front doors opened. The sound grabbed Terror's focus and he prepared himself for a battle. He hid against the wall, peeking out through the nearby window of the office. What Terror could see was a man dressed in a suit wearing sunglasses. He was bald with a brown goatee and had a earring in his left ear. Terror wondered who the man could be. The suited man turned his focus toward the office, seeing its door opened. Terror sighed as the man approached the door.

"Damn." Terror whispered to himself.

Terror bolted from the wall standing toe to toe with the suited man. They stared at one another for several seconds. Terror had his guns out as did the suited man. They questioned each other of their identities. Their manner of dress and their demeanor was a clear cut of two distinct different forces.

"How did you get in here?" The suited man asked.

"I found a way." Terror gestured with a smirk.

"I see. I take it you now understand what must be done."

"What will be done?" I'm intrigued to know."

"I must kill you now. For trespassing on private property."

"That's not going to happen here." Terror said. "Besides, we just met."

"True. We have."

The suited man fired a shot at Terror with his pistol. Terror dodged the bullet quickly. His dodging speed fascinated the suited man who ran off with Terror following him. The two exit the laboratory and the suited man jumped into a vehicle, driving off with Terror chasing him down on the motorcycle.

II

<u>GOOD OR EVIL</u>

Terror chased the suited man through the streets of Chicago. Running past the stop signs and stop lights, the two were at a quick pace from each other. The suited man turned corners to knock Terror from his motorcycle, yet, Terror was heavily trained and equipped to maneuver the motorcycle when it came to corners and sharp turns.

"This man is agile." Terror noted.

Continuing to plow down the streets, almost running into incoming vehicles. The suited man passed by a police car and the police chase after him with Terror following. Terror is interested in seeing what actions will be taken in account between the suited man and the police officer. The officer stopped, and Terror passed him, still on track to the suited man. The officer now chased down Terror. His lights blinking and the siren roaring.

"You have to be kidding me." Terror said, looking behind him at the officer.

Terror stopped on the side of the road as did the officer. The officers exited the car and tackled Terror to the ground, handcuffing him.

"What the hell is going on?!" Terror yelled.

"You are under arrest."

"On what charges?"

"For speeding."

"What about the man you were chasing before me?"

"He will be taken care of." said the other officer.

"Doesn't look like he will."

"Shut your mouth." The officer yelled. "You're coming with us to the cell."

Terror sat in the jail cell. He already contacted a fellow friend to come and bail him out. While Terror waited for his friend to arrive, he meditated to himself. Questioning and discerning the suited man and his purpose for running away. It wasn't usual for someone of his nature to choose that form of action. Terror was certain there was more to his hastiness than a fight. An officer approached the cell, staring at Terror.

"You're out."

"Finally."

The officer unlocked the cell door, opening it for Terror to exit. Terror discerned the officer and his appearance. Terror realized that every officer started at him and it wasn't pleasant. They looked upon him as a criminal. A personal criminal to Chicago.

"Just to let you know." The officer whispered. "You're no better than those nubreed freaks."

Terror watched the officer walk away and his friend approach him from the front door. Carl Prater is his name and he has been a close ally to Terror for many years. Since before the rising of the heroes.

"Good to see you Carl." Terror said. "What took you?"

"Some minor interferences regarding the bailout. Nothing more serious than that."

"I'm sure you're going to question me on why I was placed in here."

"I am. What happened to get you in jail?"

"I'll explain in the car." Terror said.

"Alright."

Terror entered Carl's vehicle. A small average car. Not to exploiting to others on the road. Carl preferred the simple as does Terror. Carl drove down the road to return to their base. Carl looked over to Terror, seeing him focused. Completely focused.

"What is it now?"

"I need to find that man in the suit." Terror replied. "There's something going on in the city that I'm unaware of."

"My friend, there's plenty going on which you're unaware of. Think of that guy going around at night."

"You're talking about me, aren't you?"

"Actually, I'm not." Carl said with a laugh. "I'm talking about the devil figure that was roaming some time ago."

"He's still around."

"How do you know?"

"Saw him the night I went after The Party People."

"Speaking of them, what happened up in Canada?"

"You would like to know wouldn't you."

"That's why I asked." Carl continued. "Tell me, did you meet him?"

"Meet who?"

"You know who I'm talking about."

"You have to be very specific." Terror gestured. "There were quite a few I met up there."

"The Swordman." Carl yelled. "Did you meet him?"

"I did."

"So, he's real."

"Yes, Carl. The Swordman exists."

Carl was delighted to know of The Swordman's existence. After reading about the sightings of others such as The Swordman roaming across the world. Carl was highly interested in this new age of sightings. Particularly of gods, heroes, titans, and even monsters and phantoms. Terror on the other hand, only looked at it as another phase in life to encounter in the future. Whether it may be to fight against or to align himself with. It made no difference to him.

'This is great to hear."

"You want to meet him?" Terror asked with humor. "You can tell me."

"Of course, I want to meet him. He's the main talk of these rising figure. these folkloric entities roaming the world. Come on, you mean to tell me you didn't feel anything when you met him?"

"When we met, we fought. That was our first encounter."

"You fought him?"

"He was dealing with The Party People. I came in to rid them and he was in the way.”

“You two aren’t on opposite terms, are you?”

“We’re fine. We have separate businesses to deal with.”

“Speaking of business, there’s a woman who you need to meet.”

“What woman?”

“She is aware of your doings in the city. She wants to question you on your motives.”

“Don’t tell me you invited a reporter to the hideout.”

“I did somewhat. She’s not a reporter per say.”

“Then, what in the hell is she? An attorney? A judge? A hunter?”

“If only. Maybe she is, I didn’t ask her.”

Terror sighed. Facing the road in front of him. Carl wondered how Terror would react to seeing the woman and he will find out soon enough.

They returned to the hideout in the outskirts of Chicago. Away from the city limits. Terror paced toward the door, using his key to unlock it. Opening the door, Terror turned around and behind him was the woman standing next to Carl. Dressed in jeans, a white shirt covered with a brown jacket. Her hair was brown as sand and her countenance was bold.

“The hell she come from?” Terror wondered.

“She was already here.” Carl replied. “Figure it would be better that way.”

“You figured. Great.”

They entered the hideout. Inside was decorated with an armory of tremendous weaponry. The walls ranged from guns to swords to axes to war hammers. Other shelves on the walls featured books. Aged ones from centuries before with encrypted writings upon their spines. Some were written in Latin. Others in different languages. Hebrew, Greek, Persian, and others written in the language of the supernatural. The hideout wasn't just a place to bunker, it was a place to keep evidence that the world has yet to see.

The woman walked through the hideout, which was two stories in height. She approached the bookshelves, reaching for the book with the supernatural writing on its spine. Terror caught her and stared.

"That one you should leave be." He told her, and she backed away. "Your name, miss? What is it?"

"Jordan Dodson." She said.

"And what are you supposed to be? A reporter?"

"I'm not a reporter as you would consider one such."

"Then, what are you?"

"I'm a conspiracy theorist." She replied.

"You are huh?"

"I've been called one due to my heavily influenced work on the rising events circling the world."

"You're into that stuff too."

"Can't tell me you aren't either. This stuff is magnificent compared to what we've already known."

"Heed my words, Ms. Dodson." Terror said, walking toward her. "You don't want to get too involved in the realm where gods and monsters exist. It will only bring trouble to your heart and soul.”

“So, tell me, John Terror. Why do you do what you do?”

“You’re aware of that as well?”

“I am.”

“Where did you find your information? Carl gave it to you?”

“Actually, he didn’t.”

“Then how do you know about me and what I do for my purpose?”

“I’ve been watching you for some time.” She said. “Ever since I noticed the crime rate go down. I knew there was something happening in the city and one night. I saw you. On your motorcycle. Blazing down criminals with your own weapons. It was fascinating to actually see someone such as yourself doing what I believe to be a great cause.”

“You find my actions to be great?”

“I do. The same goes for the others throughout the world. The one in Canada. The other in Enigma City. All of them. They’re doing these things not for self-indulgence or selfish motives. They aspire to help others such as myself and in doing so, inspiring them to become greater. To get out of their own way and establish a broader sense of reality.”

“You really believe that?” Terror asked. “Seriously? Out of their own way to establish some form of good in this world?”

“That’s exactly what I believe. What other purpose could they possibly have to not do such a thing?”

“Many reasons, Ms. Dodson.”

“And you would be aware of them?”

"I am. Which is why I prefer to work alone in the field. It keeps me calm and the business is done. No interruptions and no changes. all flows as it should, and the deed will be completed."

"How can you be so sure?"

"Because my work proves it." Terror declared. "How else can you see the coming change if not without the work."

"Good point." Jordan said. "So, you're seriously about all of this? Completely in?

"Yes."

Jordan stepped closer toward Terror. Unsure of her motives, Terror moved a step away. Jordan noticed him and nodded with a smile. Terror nodded and gestured his hand for Jordan to respond as he knew she was going to. Carl only watched them and wondered what was going on truly.

"I see." Jordan said as she walked toward the door. "But, before I decide to go, I hope, truly, I hope there's something more that comes from your work in Chicago. More hero worthy."

"Hero worthy?"

"Yes. Worth of a hero. You'll deserve it if your motives are indeed true."

"My work is what it is." Terror said. "It will speak for itself."

"I know."

Jordan left through the door with Carl staring at Terror. He approached him, gesturing his attention between Terror and the door. Terror watched him as he moved his head continually back and forth. He chuckled seeing Carl's slightly known motives.

"What is it?"

"Nothing." Carl said. "Nothing at all. Just."

"Just what?" Terror asked. "I can tell you want to say something and it's about her."

"It is about her. How could you just let her leave? You saw how pretty she was."

"What does it have to do with the work at hand? The dealings with these criminals and this suited man at the laboratory hidden from public sight?"

"Honestly, nothing."

"Why bring it up?"

"Because, we haven't seen a woman as interested in this stuff in a long time. Not since Jade."

'Best not to speak about Jade." Terror said, holding his hand up to Carl."

"Gotcha." Carl said with a little haste.

The suited man approached a metal door. He looked back, seeing nothing but the wilderness behind him. The door slid open and he entered. Inside was a manufacturing facility instilled with a scientific area. Detailed with laboratories, offices, and medical rooms. The suited man walked through the area, passing by scientists and technicians. One technician approached the suited man with a salute.

"Where is the boss?" The suited man asked.

"In his office, sir."

"Thank you."

The suited man went toward the office and knocked on the door. The door opened and inside was sitting an older man at his desk. He was bald, clean-shaved and wore a pair of glasses that shaded his eyes from the sight of others. He looked up toward the suited man and smiled.

"You've made it back."

"Yes sir. I figured it was of my best intensions."

"Indeed, it was. How was the laboratory in Chicago?"

"It was intact. Except for one particular problem."

"What problem did you manage to find?" The elder man asked with interest.

"There was a man inside the lab. He was searching through the files in your office."

"Was he now?"

"Yes sir."

"And what was this man's apparel?"

"What do you mean?"

"How was he dressed? Did he have any insignias on his clothing? Did he carry with him any weapons of any kind?"

"He wore all black with some kind of design on his chest. The letter T to be exact. Detailed as a skull."

"I know of this design."

"You do? How?"

"Because only the vigilante of Chicago bears that mark."

"You're speaking of this 'John Terror' individual?"

"I am." He said keenly.

"What do you propose we do about him, Professor?"

"Find him and bring him here."

"I can do that, sir."

"No need, Agent 51. I will send Hunter Vazquez to find John Terror."

"Are you sure his anger won't cloud his mission?"

"His anger will aid him. Besides, John Terror and Hunter Vazquez have a history that needs a little rekindling."

Outside of the facility, Hunter Vazquez stood, staring at the wilderness while smoking a cigarette. He took a breather, dropping the cigarette and stomping it into the dirt. Vazquez fixed his clothing, all black with a black trench coat, similar to Terror. Vazquez placed his sunglasses over his eyes and walked over to his motorcycle. Vazquez rode off from the facility.

III

HUNTER SEEKS THE PREY

Terror returned to the laboratory as nightfall approached. Carl went along with him. Upon making their way toward the lab, they hear a car coming behind them. Both turned, seeing the car and as it stopped, Jordan exited. Carl laughed, Terror only hung his head, taking gestures toward Jordan.

"Why are you here?" Terror asked.

"I figured it would be something worth wile if I came along with the two of you."

"How did you even know we were here?"

"Carl sent me the address through a text."

"Oh, he did. Did he?" Terror said, glaring a hole through Carl.

"She can be of some help to us." Carl said. "I mean, she has a track record of this kind of stuff."

"Not a record similar to mine or even your short one."

"I may not. But, I am of some use to you regarding all of this mystery."

"Look, Ms. Dodson. If you want to deal with conspiracy, I suggest you make a trip up north. There's plenty of them there to discover."

"There's one here and I intend on uncovering it. With your help."

Terror sighed. Taking turns to Carl and Jordan. He reluctant nodded as he allowed them to follow. They followed him to the same entry point where he previously came. The door still unlocked as they entered. Inside, the area was silent as before. Only with the slight chill in the air from the outside temperature. Terror held his hand close to his firearm on his waist. Carl walked closely to Terror, knowing he'll strike first if they were to be attacked. Jordan walked with them, carrying a notebook in her hand. She wrote down everything she could see. To study it later.

"Did you manage to find the owner of this place?" She asked Terror.

"No. I've never even encountered the owner. Only his pawn I believe."

"That suited fellow you kept talking about?" Carl asked.

"Who else was I referring to?"

"Could've been anyone, my friend. You know how many men these days dress in tight suits and wear cool shades."

"He wasn't what you would call 'cool'. He was more mysterious in nature. Unsure of his motives as of my own."

"He's just like you?" Jordan asked. "Is that what you're telling us?"

"No. We've different. But, our intents are similar in nature. We strive to accomplish our goals. Whatever the costs."

"But, why are we here? I mean, did he manage to leave something behind for you to return and pick up?"

"No. I want to take another look at those files."

"What files?" Carl asked hesitantly. "You never mentioned anything about some files."

"For good reason. The files contained names and details of other nubreeds across Chicago. I need to make sure they're not being targeted like many others in secret."

"You care about them?"

Terror stared at Jordan for a split moment. He took her words in and only replied with a nod before focusing his attention toward the office he was in before. Terror entered the office and the files were sitting where he left them. He grabbed them in haste and handed them to Carl to hold.

"Take care of them."

"I will."

Searching for more information, Jordan examined a few of the files, she wrote down the names written on the tabs and recorded them in her notebook. They intrigued her heavily and she kept writing down as much information as she could regarding each individual file. Carl was impressed with her ethic as was Terror, who watched her for a moment.

"She has spirit." he said.

"Yes, I do." Jordan smiled to Terror.

Terror searched the office desks and the shelves for more information. Not finding any, he turned to Carl and Jordan. Both were in depth with the files. Terror knew they had to leave, regardless if anything else was hidden in the office. He had what he came for and was done.

"Best we leave."

"Are you sure?" Carl asked.

"I'm sure. I have a slight feeling something's about to take place."

"You mean a premonition?" Jordan asked with interest.

"You can call it that."

"Don't worry about it." Carl said. "He's had these feelings for as long as he can remember. Not many of them come to pass. Not many."

The glass windows near the office shattered with a loud cracking boom. Carl and Jordan ducked, and Terror stood his ground. From the glass rose a figure dressed in all black with black sunglasses. His brown skin could be seen from the office. Terror knew who he was staring at. Carl and Jordan on the other hand, were unsure of the whole scene.

"I knew you would be back!" Vazquez yelled. "How are you, John?!"

"Who the hell is that?!" Carl yelled.

"Hunter Vazquez." Terror answered. "I know of him from times past."

"How do you know him?" Jordan asked.

"It's a long story. To be told another time."

Vazquez stood outside of the office, gesturing Terror to step out and fight. Terror knew he had to fight and he turned to Carl and Jordan, glaring at the files. He looked around and found another exit only a few feet from the office was only.

"Carl, do you see the exit over there?"

"I do."

"You and Jordan get out of here and return to base."

"What about you?"

"I'll deal with Vazquez. I have to." Terror said, removing his trench coat. He handed the coat over to Carl, standing his ground.

"You got it, boss." Carl said as he and Jordan ran out of the office toward the exit."

"I'll find you back at the base." Terror said, watching Carl and Jordan exit.

"It's just you and me, old friend." Vazquez remarked.

Terror ran toward Vazquez, who done the same. Both men clashed into one another with shoulder tackles. Terror snatched Vazquez by his collar and delivered a series of punches to his face, shattering his sunglasses. Vazquez only laughed off the pain as he chocked Terror and slammed him into one of the nearby medical tables. The force of the choke slam cracked the table with Terror atop. He caught his breath for the moment and Vazquez grabbed him, holding him up in the air. Vazquez tossed Terror through the glass window to the outside. Terror shook his head, he looked around, now realizing he's outside. He took another breather before standing up. Terror stood while Vazquez approached him with quickening steps.

"I will not give up." Terror said. "You know I won't."

"I do. But, there's no need for you to surrender so easily."

Terror punched and kicked Vazquez, but his body was able to absorb the attacks. Vazquez grabbed Terror by the throat and head butted him. Terror fell to the ground, unconscious. Vazquez chuckled under his breath looking down at the collapsed Terror.

"You're tougher than this." He mentioned. "How could you ever have before so still and so simple-minded to your purpose."

Vazquez carried Terror over his shoulder, placing him into a van which bore the logo of Agency X. Vazquez entered the van and drove off from the facility. Intent on taking him to his boss.

IV

<u>WHAT CAN YOU BECOME?</u>

Vazquez reached the wilderness far out from the city. Terror still unconscious, laying in the back of the van. Vazquez approached the facility. Large in its structure and surrounded by militiamen and doctors. Vazquez drove pass the entrance, heading toward the parking entry point. Stopping the van, Vazquez gathered other militiamen to assist him in carrying terror out of the van and into the facility. They carried and somewhat dragged Terror inside and toward a table. The doctors took Terror and laid him atop the table. They examined him and cleared him for the next step which was to be raised up for further inspection. After they hung him up by his arms and legs, he awoke. Finding himself in the facility and tied to the hanging table. In front of him stood Vazquez with the suited man and his boss. An elderly man wearing glasses.

"Where in the hell am I?" Terror asked.

"You're where you belong." the Professor replied. "With us. Your real allies in this world."

"My real allies?"

"Precisely. I am aware you and Vazquez have known each other for some time, and it felt best to have him bring you here. Just for me to see you."

"What's so important about me?"

'Everything, John Terror." The Professor said with a smile. "Everything."

"You cannot be serious, sir." Vazquez mentioned. "He's just a pawn in the field. Waiting to be taken for the prey he has become."

'Hold your tongue, Hunter Vazquez. There are still many things about John Terror that I must know."

"As of what?"

"Your nubreed genes. Your skills in combat and most importantly, your connection to the spiritual world."

Terror stared at the Professor, who grinned toward him. Waiting to hear more from Terror's mouth. Terror knew he had to find a way to escape but was trapped by the hanging table and the tow doors guarded by Vazquez and Agent 51. Terror attempted to pull his arms from the scaffold, yet, they were tied tightly by the chains. Vazquez mocked him.

"You want to get out of here don't you?" Vazquez gestured.

"Only after I sever your head from your body."

"I can't wait for it."

The Professor turned to Vazquez and Agent 51.

"Leave me with John Terror.'

"Why?" Agent 51 asked. "What if something goes wrong? You need us in here with you. By your side for protection."

"I will be perfectly fine." The Professor declared. "Trust me."

The two guardsmen left the lab. The Professor walked toward Terror, staring up at him. Terror stared by, but with only the intent of finding his way down and out. The Professor rubbed his chin, mediating on the questions he desired to ask Terror.

"I know you wish to ask me some questions. Please, do so before I move on to mine."

"What is this place?"

"This place is of one facility dedicated to discovering the true purpose of the nubreeds. It is why Agency X was created."

"This is Agency X?"

"Yes. Founded by yours truly and other men who aren't here to attend this rare occasion. But, Agency X does exist, and it operates under the eyes and ears of Man."

"More secret societies." Terror scoffed. "How great."

"We're not those kinds of groups. We're something greater. Far more special than any other mere allegiance."

"Then, why am I here? Truly."

"You're here because I wanted to meet you."

'Meet me?"

"Yes. I've heard about your record of stopping criminal activity in Chicago. As I know of your ventured into Canada to find The Party People and apparently, you ended up as an ally of The Swordman. Partially gaining his trust."

"How do you know of this?"

"We have our eyes and ears in every location known for a nubreed sighting. Or those that pertain to folkloric figures such as the ones you met up north. We've managed to capture some. But, their genes weren't strong enough for our procedures."

"You're saying you killed them?"

"Yes. They had to die. No need to continue living upon the earth as weak and void as they were."

"Is that why you wish to know about my connection to the spirit world?", To communicate with the dead and the powers they possess?"

"I want to siphon that power from you and open a portal into that world. I believe the spirit world and all that lies within it may contain great power that will make us gods among the men."

Terror laughed gently. The Professor could only stare at Terror's glimmering smile. He was glad to see it. Terror stared at the Professor and nodded.

"I never got your name." Terror said. "They've only called your boss."

"My name is Professor Mite."

"Mite. Huh, like a gnat or a flee."

"I am not. My name signifies power to come. A great power."

"You're delusional. Blinded by your desire for power you cannot wield or obtain under human reach. You'll destroy yourself before having a glimpse at the power you crave."

"We'll see about that." The Professor said, exiting the lab.

Back at Terror's base, Carl and Jordan looked at a map on the table. They signaled a possible trace to find Terror. Carl is aware he would leave marks wherever he was before moving on to another location. Carl was certain Terror left something behind at the laboratory to give them a chance at finding him.

"Are you sure we can find him?" Jordan asked. "He hasn't come back in hours."

"Which means he's been taken and I'm sure he left something for us to find. He always does."

"Now where do you think he left something for us to trace?"

"Simple. Back at the creepy lab."

Terror remained in his current predicament. He raised his head seeing Vazquez and Agent 51 entering the room. He wondered and waited for them to say something. They only stared at him with malicious intent on their mind. They wanted him dead. Believing he was pulling the Professor astray from the Agency's purpose.

"You're just going to stand there?"

"We don't like you." Vazquez said.

"I can see."

"I should've killed you when we first met."

"And what do they call you? I know it isn't 'The Suited Man'. At least, I hope it isn't."

"I am Agent 51 of Agency X. Loyal to the cause and to Professor Mite."

"Agent 51? What happened to the other fifty?"

"Nothing that concerns you."

"Why is he here." Vazquez said to Agent 51. "We can kill him now."

"We could. But, there are other methods we can use to turn his mind on himself. Therefore, allowing him to kill himself."

"Nothing greater than killing your enemy with your own hands."

"I'm aware of your experience in the field, Vazquez."

"Why does your Professor want me anyway?" Terror asked. "I know you're both aware of the situation."

"Should we tell him?" Agent 51 asked.

"What else are we here for?"

"You're here to be recruited into the fold."

"You mean, to align with the both of you?" Terror laughed. "I would rather be dead than take the offer."

"You wouldn't be aware of the cause. The Professor is preparing to have your mind renewed and cleansed before handing you the offer. He wants a pure mind in his squadron."

"As I said, I would rather be dead. Better to kill myself than join in your pawn ranking system."

"This isn't the time to play the fool!" Vazquez said, lunging toward Terror their eyes locked onto one another. Both are willing to fight to the death. Agent 51 could only watch the scene and he was in timid fear of his place in the room. Vazquez came own from the table and walked out of the door. Agent 51 followed him out with Terror shaking his head and sighing.

Carl and Jordan returned to the lab. They entered through the shattered window. Carl remembered the window was previously in place before they left and the other one is where Vazquez busted in.

"Someone was tossed through here."

"How can you be sure of that?" Jordan asked.

"Something had to be thrown out. Either Terror or that guy."

Inside, they searched for anything that could lead back to Terror and upon walking on the floor, Carl noticed something shining. He ran over and kneeled. Removing the shattered glass and debris from the object, he discovered a handheld object. As small as a pocket box and black as coal. It blinked with a white light. Carl gasped.

"What?" Jordan said walking toward him.

"This has to be it."

Jordan looked at the object. She wasn't sure what it could be. Yet, saw the eagerness in Carl's eyes.

"Are you sure?"

"I am. Not many possess this kind of technology in Chicago."

"And where did Terror end up getting this thing?"

"From one of his previous experiences. Dealt with entering a Hawke Industries building. He'll explain it to you another time."

"Now, how does this help us find him?"

"Give me a moment."

Carl continued tampering with the object and from the blinking light arose a holographic map. The map detailed a trail between the facility they stood in and another one far in the wilderness. Jordan looked out of the window and spotted Terror's bike on the side of the building and tire tracks in the dirt.

"He didn't take the bike with him."

Carl saw the bike outside while Jordan returned dot the outside, measuring at the tire tracks. Carl followed her and saw the tracks himself.

"They took him." Carl said.

"Whoever did, these tracks can help us find out where they've taken him."

"Then, let's get to it."

Carl used the device as they tracked down the tire tracks.

The Professor returned to the room and brought Terror down to his eye level. The Professor stared at him. As if he was studying him like a test subject and Terror could sense it well. Vazquez and Agent 51 returned to the room, staring at Terror.

"You brought him lower." Vazquez said.

" I need a closer look at him." The Professor said. "Better that way to study subjects."

"Sir, myself and Vazquez have come to a conclusion regarding John Terror."

"What have you conjured in your minds to meld together?"

"We kill him." Vazquez declared. "Get rid of him now and be done with this."

The Professor laughed as he turned toward his two guardsmen. Terror was unsure what was taking place as he struggled to get loose with all his intensions.

"I will not signal his death. I understand you want him dead, Vazquez. But, he is important to the Agency."

"The Agency or to yourself?" Agent 51 asked.

"I truth, to both. Terror possesses something neither of you have in your strength and it is required of myself and the Agency to have that power."

"You speak of his connection to the spirits?"

"Yes. Can either of you contact or enter the spirit world?"

"I cannot." Agent 51 nodded.

"I once could." Vazquez said. "But, John stole it from me. He took a lot from many of us in the past days."

"It went to whoever desired it, Vazquez." Terror said. "Better you take another look at your past."

"You disgust me."

"As do you." Terror grinned.

Vazquez lunged and grabbed Terror by his throat. He prepared himself to kill him as claws appeared from his fingertips. His urge called for Terror's death and he now has the chance.

"Vazquez stand down!" The Professor yelled.

Vazquez growled in Terror's face. He wanted him dead and he knows have the chance to do it. The Professor stepped to Vazquez's side. Looking at the fury in his eyes and the mockery in Terror's. Agent 51 reached for his gun hidden in his coat. just in case something goes wrong.

"Let him go."

"He needs to die, Professor." Vazquez yelled. "He can't continue to live being the man he is."

"Go ahead, Vazquez." Terror said. "You have your change."

"Vazquez! Don't take heed to his words! Ignore them. Listen to me and I will have settled all of this."

Vazquez shook his head. Torn between obeying his boss or following what sat in his heart. His right hand went into the air, ready to strike.

"I can't let him live."

Vazquez swiped his claw toward Terror. Terror shook himself, allowing Vazquez to slash through the chains on his arm. The chains snapped. Terror's arms were free. Terror smiled and punched Vazquez. Agent 51 fired shots toward Terror. Terror stumbled from the shots and stared at Agent 51. He smiled as the bullets fell from his chest and the wounds healed.

"The hell was that?!" Agent 51 yelled.

"Something I was born with." Terror smiled.

The Professor stared at Terror's healing wounds. Intrigued and excited at the same time. He's never encountered such an individual in his time as a professor. He knew the age had changed.

"Fascinating."

Terror broke through the chains on his legs. Stepping off the platform with a stumble. Terror lunged toward Agent 51, smashing his head through a window. The Agent fell while Vazquez stood and faced Terror. The two locked eyes and lunged toward each other. The Professor stormed out of the room as the two former allies fought.

Carl and Jordan arrived outside the facility, seeing the gated entrance.

"How are we going to find a way in?"

"There's a way." Carl said. "You'll see."

Terror and Vazquez bolted from the room, breaking the door from its hinges and fought on the floor with the scientists fleeing the scene. Soldiers attempted to break them up yet overpowered by the combined strength of the two men. The commotion gathered everyone from outside, leaving the entrance unchecked.

Carl saw everyone running toward the facility.

"Now's our chance!"

They went through the gate quietly while seeing the soldiers storming toward the facility.

"What's happening?" Jordan asked.

"Terror probably started some shit." Carl replied. "He does that."

The soldiers circled the brawl with Vazquez threw Terror into the soldiers. They picked him up and shoved him to Vazquez, who knocked him to the floor. They were no longer interested in stopping them. It became a fight club for the soldiers, and they relished the scene. The Professor and Agent 51 ran toward the outside where a helicopter sat.

Carl and Jordan entered and within several feet, they saw Terror and Vazquez surrounded by the soldiers fighting one another. The scene reminded Jordan of breakouts at rallies and the riots circling the world. She was disgusted by the sight of seeing mere soldiers enjoying the fighting.

"You don't like it?" Carl said.

"You can tell."

"Yeah. It's showing."

He watched and thought. He was developing a plan to get Terror out of the building. What he needed was some insight into how. He looked around while hearing the cheers of the soldiers with the sound of punches and kicks from Terror and Vazquez's brutal fight. Jordan looked around and what she spotted were canisters. The canisters were filled with oil connected to the machines running most of the facility's electrical grid.

"What about those?" She pointed.

"That could work." Carl replied. "If only there was a way to blow them up."

They though and stared at the soldiers, seeing firearms attached to their belts.

Terror and Vazquez continued their brawl. Both were tired and their wounds continually healing. Yet, slowing down due to the lack of energy. They exhaled roughly as the soldiers egged them on to continue fighting.

"They want us to kill one another." Terror said.

"Better that way." Vazquez replied. "You will be dead."

They lunged toward each other, this time falling into the crowd of soldiers and near the canisters. Carl and Jordan raced down to reach the area. Rattling one another with swipes, punches, kicks, and haymakers, both men were worn out and they fell to their knees.

"You believe this will settle things?" Terror asked. "That this will end all that happened in the past?"

"With you gone from this world? Yes. It will solve many things."

"Still the fool."

Terror snatched a gun from a nearby soldier and shot Vazquez in the chest. He fell to the floor and the room silenced. Carl and Jordan stopped and could only stare, seeing Terror standing tall, holding the gun in his hand. He scoffed before facing the soldiers and firing rounds at them. He killed as many as he could. Carl and Jordan ran to assist him.

"John!" Carl yelled. "John, we're here!"

Terror looked and saw Carl and Jordan coming. He nodded before fighting off the soldiers. They reached him as the soldiers plotted out a plan to kill them.

"Are you alright?"

"I'm fine." Terror said. "We need to get out of here."

"We have an idea."

Terror looked, and Carl gestured for the gun. Terror turned his head toward the canisters and he understood.

"Let me do it." Terror said.

"Are you sure?"

"Trust me, I'll make it out alive."

"Gotcha."

Carl and Jordan ran out of the facility while Terror turned to the canisters and fired a shot. The shot shook the canisters as each of them exploded. Carl and Jordan were outside when they heard the explosion. In the air, the Professor and Agent 51 saw the explosion from the helicopter.

"He's free." Agent 51 said.

"We have what we need." The Professor replied, holding a chrome briefcase on his lap as the helicopter flew from the scene. Carl managed to catch a glimpse of the helicopter before it vanished the scene. They saw the facility blow up into pieces with the flames in the sky. As the explosion settled, they saw a figure walking out of the facility and through the fire.

"There he is." Carl said.

Jordan was startled as she saw Terror walking out of the facility and through the flames. Unburned and his clothes not scorched. He reached them and nodded with a slight exhale.

"I saw a helicopter leave as the explosion happened." Carl mentioned.

"He escaped. I figured he would. Let's get out of here before the feds arrive."

They returned to their base and a week had passed. No word of the Professor, Agent 51, or Vazquez was mentioned through the thick air of the criminal underworld. No mention or sighting of anything related to Agency X. Jordan had decided to assist Terror and Carl in their endeavors while learning more about the world and what is truly happening across it. Terror searched and there were no leads to finding any of them. He knew they were still in operation, just somewhere else far from Chicago. Relieved for the moment, he returned to stopping criminal activity in the city.

While cleaning up the streets, Terror encountered someone who was aware of Agency X's whereabouts and what they intend to do with Chicago and many other cities across the world. Terror took the notes and later found a facility where men who claimed to work for the Agency resided on their business trip.

Terror entered their lair and defeated them in hand-to-hand combat. The fight went outside behind the residence. There, Terror took the opportunity to interrogate the group of men. Their uniforms caught Terror's attention as they bore the logo of Agency X on their clothing, they gave Terror no details on where the Agency was kept nor of what their current and future plans hold. Terror decided in killing them because of their uselessness. After killing them, Terror found himself staring at Kenari Clark, dressed in a mixture of casual and business apparel. Yet, he managed to spot the insignia of the Creed of Swords on the left side of his jacket.

"I'll be damn." Terror said. "Been a while and yet, I see you again."

Intrigued to know why he came down from Retropolis to Chicago. Reminded him of his previous venture.

"It was only a matter of time." Kenari said.

Both men shook hands. Remembering their deal in Retropolis. Kenari came to Terror with a proposal in mind. One that will require many hands to protect the world from a coming threat. A threat neither of them could handle on their own.

Q-ARROW: QUANTUM PLANS

I

THE QUANTUM PLOY

From his aftermath with the Hitman, Asher Dale continued to run his company, Quantum Industries. The past few days have caught Asher for the number of articles pertaining toward the mystery of the Q-Arrow. Asher loved the attention his alter-ego was receiving and wasn't banking on it to cease. Once he leaves the Quantum office, he moved toward his owned casinos. Taking in the moments of its visitors gambling on the machines and relishing in the luxuries his casinos provided for them.

"I love this." Asher said, watching the crowds of people in his casino.

On the other side of Asher's fortunes are those who desire to bring him and his empire down. Ranging from the black-market deals concerning his casinos and the information reliable to his company. Asher continued to fight them off with his Q-Arrow persona. The black market had begun to fear the presence of the Quantum Archer as he's been referred to by those of the market.

Asher returned home to find Jarvis Hoyt waiting for him in his office. Jarvis continually watched over Asher's other duties while he's out in the day with the city's people.

"What's come up now?"

"Nothing on that Hitman fellow if you were thinking."

"He's still a problem for us. I'm not ceasing on going calm with him."

"There's other things that require your attention."

"Such as?"

"There's word of someone within the black market who's making their way toward Las Vegas. To confront the Q-Arrow personally."

"That's a first." Asher remarked.

"Be that as it may, it will cause a problem for the city. Just like the Hitman did to gain your attention."

"What do you propose we do?"

"I'll keep my eye out on this foreign invader while you manage to keep your double-life a secret."

"What else now?"

"Karen's been researching things on the Q-Arrow ever since the Hitman incident."

"Just tell her to stop."

"Not my duty." Jarvis smirked. "That's your department."

Asher sighed off the notice while Jarvis had left.

Meanwhile, Karen Harp went into deeper research of the Q-Arrow. So far, she's learned about his weaponry and a few of his tactics. She's not impressed by how he postures himself before the city. She had begun a quick study on the Hitman incident, discovering some security camera footage of the two confronting one another. She tried to understand Q-Arrow's motives toward the Hitman. She could not. Finding herself lost in the mystery of Q-Arrow's existence and purpose.

"There has to be something."

Karen looked over, hearing her cell phone ringing. She stood up from the desk to grab the phone and it was Asher calling her.

"Strange enough for you to call."

"It's important."

"How so?"

"Jarvis told me you're researching the Q-Arrow."

"I am."

"It's best you don't. For your own protection."

"Protection from who?"

"Those who seek to do him harm. If they find out you're researching him, they'll come for you as leverage to him. It won't end well for either side if it comes to that."

"Thank you for caring about me, Asher. But, you already know I can handle myself in dire situations."

"I know." Asher said calmly. "Just, be careful. Please."

"I will. No need to worry yourself over me." Karen hung up the call.

She went back to the desk and continued her research. Asher remained in his office, looking out of the window as the city of Vegas. Waiting for the sun to set and the moon to rise.

Entering the city of Las Vegas was a man. Around Asher's age and was very distinctive from his appearance and stature. His light brown hair was scruffy and wavy. Its length passed his shoulders.

Wearing a worn-out coat with dirty jeans and a buttoned shirt. The man is Sam Weyman and he entered the city, carrying with him a duffle bag. He looked around and took in the air of the city. Seeing the lights upon the buildings and the crowds of people on the Vegas Strip.

"This is their domain. Excellent."

RISING OF THE STALKER

Night had fallen upon Sin City and Weyman had found a way into the Quantum headquarters. He saw the clean white floors decorated with its white/gold walls. Almost of a heavenly appearance to the eyes of its visitors. Weyman focused himself and moved toward the laboratories. He ran for them and as he came closer, he stopped. Staring at a large churning machine. Its height stood about fifteen to twenty feet. Metallic in its rigid appearance, shining to silver. The machine had a low-volume roar as it moved on its own. Self-operating. Within the machine was energy. Quantum energy.

"This is it." Weyman said ecstatically.

Dropping his duffle bag on the floor, he opened it and pulled out a gun. A proto-absorber. One now familiar to the public, because Weyman had built it himself. His intellect and time of study allowed him to manufacture an object of such obscure scale. He aimed his gun toward the machine and fired. The machine's roar started to grow as the gun was absorbing the machine's quantum energy slowly. Weyman didn't have much patience when it came to receive what he claims to own. The machine, feeling itself being attacked had signaled a silent alarm.

Asher sat up from his desk in his lair, hearing the alarm go off. He opened the map of the location as Jarvis entered the lair.

"What's going on?"

"Something triggered the alarm back at the office." Asher said. "I'm searching to see where the alarm was triggered to begin with."

Opening a digital map of the headquarters' layout, Asher ran through the map and found the trace of the alarm coming from the laboratory sections. Preferably in the lab where the quantum machine is located. Unsure, Asher suits up in his Q-Arrow gear and leaves the lair.

Weyman continued to absorb the energy and the alarm goes off loudly. Startling Weyman. He jumped and paused the absorption process. He looked at the gun's heated range and grinned.

"Lucky me. It's enough to start with."

Weyman turned around to leave and came a shadow moving across the white floors from above. Weyman could make out the hood and the bow. Q-Arrow had arrived at the scene.

"Time for my second plan." Weyman pulled out his phone and dialed a number. "Your turn."

Q-Arrow entered through a ceiling window, running toward the laboratory. Barging through the door, he found the machine still churning. The room is left the same as it was. Q-Arrow was unclear about the alarm.

"What did you find?" Jarvis said from the comms.

"There's no one here."

"What do you mean?"

"I mean there's nothing here that could've caused the alarm."

"There's nothing wrong with the system, Asher. Something had to have triggered it."

While searching the laboratory, Q-Arrow heard the lab doors open behind him. He felt a heavy presence behind him. Turning around slowly to see, he found himself confronted by three men. Brute figures. They wore similar uniforms that appeared to be militia-based. Their faces covered with brown and black masks.

"Looks like I've found the cause." Q-Arrow said to Jarvis.

"Like what?"

"Three men. Three big men."

"Three? Who are they?"

"I'm about to ask." Q-Arrow stepped forward. "Who are you three?"

"They call me Stampede and these are my brothers, Smasher and Demolition. We are the Dominate Trio."

"You look the part. I'll give you that much credit."

"We're here on business." Smasher said. "Someone paid us to be here to stop you."

"Who is your boss?"

"You'll meet him soon. If you manage to live after the beating we give you."

Q-Arrow drew back his bow with three arrows aimed for the Trio. They didn't flinch at the sight of the arrows. Jarvis, back at the lair could only hear the drawing of the bow. He sighed.

"Best you tell me his name and leave before the three of you have an arrow in your chests."

"We're being paid a high sum to keep silent. We won't speak because of your petty threats."

"Let's just kill him." Demolition roared.

"I wouldn't do that."

Stampede gave his partners a look. The three nodded and began to step forward toward Q-Arrow. He fired the arrows, hitting the three in the chests. They paused. Laughing as they pulled the arrows from their chests. Q-Arrow only stared as the arrows clamored to the floor.

"The hell are you guys made of?"

"A great power. We'll have more when we've been paid our sum."

They moved closer to Q-Arrow and a smoke bomb fell from the ceiling, exploding on the floor. The Trio coughed and waved their arms to rid of the smoke. Q-Arrow scanned the room and what he saw was another figure. Slim. Almost his height. The figure had long straight hair and his face was covered by a black and white mask. The figure fought the Trio on his own one-by-one. The Trio ran out of the lab due to the unknown attacks and the increase of smoke.

"Who are you?" Q-Arrow asked.

"Call me Jeff Nero. I'm new to this occupation. Trust me, I won't stop after meeting you."

"You appear to be a young man. Why choose this kind of field to work in?"

"I have my reasons. Plus, I can take care of myself."

Nero vanished from the lab with a bright spark of light. Disappearing almost ninja-like leaving Q-Arrow impressed. He left the headquarters and outside, Weyman was watching. He witnessed the whole scene. Rubbing his absorber gun in hand. He put the gun back in the duffle bag amongst notes he had taken from the desks in the laboratory.

The following morning, the headquarters incident was all over the news. Karen sought the incident as the perfect opportunity to study up on Q-Arrow's doing in the city. Asher talked with Jarvis in his office at the headquarters detailing the night's event. Jarvis was uncomfortable with a young man going around the city as some form of hero. Calling him a vigilante.

"I'm one as well." Asher laughed.

"Yet, you have a reason for all of this. This young man you encountered, there's no telling why he's doing it."

"Perhaps when he comes up again, you an talk to him. Maybe set some reason in him."

"I'll give him more than some words of reason. He should be doing things others his age are doing."

"Maybe, he wants to be different. Away from the crowds of society."

"Maybe so."

"Anything on Karen?" Asher asked.

"She's actually been reading up on the incident from last night since the news broadcasted it."

"I'll talk to her."

"I thought you already had done that?" Jarvis noticed. "You're haven't?

"Not yet." Asher stood up. "I'll be back in about an hour. Maybe two."

Asher left his desk and exited the office.

Weyman visited a small facility in the outskirts of the city. He entered the building, seeing it's a facility owned by Quantum Industries. Filled with other smaller equipment related to the machine. He grinned.

"This will do as well."

Weyman pulled out the notes and used the smaller machines in the building. Mixing it with the energy he absorbed, he built a transfer system as he called it. He walked into it and on his clothing was several pieces of leaves and bark. He stepped into the energy's waves and two security guards had stepped in, seeing him. They raised up their firearms.

"Who are you?" They asked.

Weyman didn't care. He laughed as he could feel the energy entering his body and his bloodstream.

"Prepare to witness change before your very eyes!" Weyman yelled.

He screamed and from there, the energy waves formed a bright explosion occurred and from the explosion, Weyman walked out. No longer a human after society's mindset. He stared at the guards and stretched his arm toward them. His arm had transfused into a long stalk, impaling the guards. Weyman noticed his body was able to mimic the elements of the earth. Preferably plants.

"This is good." Weyman said. "Very good."

Weyman left the facility with his footsteps resembling the sounds of trees falling to the ground.

ONE CHANCE

Asher made his way to visit Karen at her workplace. A reporter's office in the middle of Las Vegas. When Asher entered the building, everyone had paused themselves and stared at him. He was unsure of their expressions, though intriguing to an extent and continued walking. Karen sat in her office reading up on the Quantum headquarters incident as Asher knocked on the door.

"Wasn't expecting to see you here."

"I came to have a word with you."

"About what exactly?"

"You know what."

"This again." Karen sighed. "I told you I will be fine. Nothing to worry about."

"I also know you've been reading up on the incident back at the office."

"And you're not interested as to what happened?"

"I know enough. Believe me."

"How?"

"I own the company. I receive all the news and goings."

"From where?"

"I have my own sources."

"I see." Karen said slightly. "Are they in the city?"

"Where else would they be? Washington?"

"Maybe." Karen smiled. "Only you would know. And Jarvis, of course."

Asher walked up to Karen at her desk.

"Just please, leave all of this alone."

"Why don't you tell me the real reason why you want me to leave it?"

"I can't." Asher sighed, sitting down in the chair.

"You can't, or you won't?"

"Little bit of both to be honest."

Karen stood up from her desk, grabbing her purse and walking toward the door. Asher jumped up and stood in front of her. In between her and the door.

"Just listen." Asher said. "The reason I can't tell you is…"

"Is what? Just spit it out."

"I'm more than what you already know."

"I figured that out when we were children."

"I'm being honest." Asher rubbed his head. "Come by the home tonight and I'll explain everything there."

"This better not be some sexual notification you're throwing my way."

"Trust me, it's not."

Karen nodded slowly. Showing surety toward Asher's decision and he left the office. While Asher was leaving, Jarvis had called him.

"What is it?" Asher wondered.

"Apparently one of your facilities was attacked about an hour ago."

"Attacked?"

"And you know who."

"Must be whoever brought in the Trio from the lab." Asher nodded. "I'm on my way there now."

Asher had arrived at the facility with Jarvis waiting for him. The area covered with police and forensics. The news had yet to have learned about the facility's current situation. Inside, they discovered a portion of the interior was brunt and found the bodies of the two guards. Asher looked around the area and saw the remains of a built machine.

"That machine wasn't here prior to this facility."

"What are you saying?" Jarvis asked.

"Whoever did all of this had to have built that first. Explains why the wall is completely burnt to a crisp."

The forensics approached Asher and Jarvis with a sample of what they've found. Asher looked and saw it was a fragment of tree bark. Confused, he looked around for plants and there was none within the facility.

"Where did you find this again?" Jarvis asked.

"In here. Next to the machine. There were also some remnants underneath the skin of the two guards. As if they were killed by impaling of a wooden stick."

"Aren't there security cameras here?"

"We put them in here just in case of situations like this."

"Then, let's go have a look." Jarvis said.

They entered the security room and found the footage. On the footage, they saw a man walking with a duffle bag. They saw him construct the machine and they saw the explosion.

"This isn't making any sense." Jarvis said.

"A lot of things these days aren't."

After the explosion, they saw the man having been transformed into some tree-like creature and how he killed the guards. The forensics were uncertain as to what they have just seen.

"The hell was that?" Jarvis wondered.

"Something strange and something only made by the hacking of Quantum's work."

Jarvis' phone had begun to ring loudly. He opened the screen and received an emergency notice from the City of Henderson where the three-like creature had entered the city and is causing chaos.

"They're calling the creature some kind of wood-stalking figure."

"You know what we need to do." Asher said.

"Isn't it a little early for, you know, doing what't next?"

"Not when it's necessary."

Jarvis nodded. "I'll keep you posted."

Asher nodded and left the facility. Jarvis continued to speak with the forensics and officers concerning the future of the facility. While talking, Jarvis noticed a young man standing around the scene. He approached him with haste.

"Who are you?"

"Jeff Nero."

"And you are what? An officer? Forensics?"

"Neither. I'm the guy who aided the Q-Arrow in the Quantum labs. Figured he would be here."

"So, you're this ninja guy, huh?"

"How do you know about me?"

"Because," Jarvis pulled Nero aside from the officers. "I work with the Q-Arrow."

"You do? Explains why you're here. But, where is he?"

"Going to confront the one responsible."

"Then, I should be following alongside him."

"I don't think that's best for your health."

"Why not?"

"Q-Arrow has Las Vegas under control."

"Like with guys such as the Hitman showing up? You've seen what's happening around the world. There are others out there who could do more harm if they were in this city. I've read the stories and the accounts of those in Retropolis and Enigma City. Q-Arrow is not like them, he's different."

"How would you know? How would you even understand?"

"My age doesn't matter. I've had enough experience to know what's right and wrong. Me helping Q-Arrow is what's right."

Jarvis sighed. He rubbed his head and stared at the young man.

"You're still young. You can have a life. A life better than chasing after some hero's dream."

"A hero's dream is all I need to do a bit of good in this world. Living for myself won't cut it. Hell, it won't even solve any problem that I will face."

"You're different than most youngsters I've met."

"So I've been told."

"I'll tell you where Q-Arrow is going, but, you have to make sure you keep this information to yourself."

"Understood."

Asher returned to his home as the afternoon had begun to settle down. He grabbed his Q-Arrow gear and prepared to get suited up, until he saw Karen standing by the front door. He sighed. Putting down the torso gear.

"Shit."

Asher went to the front door and opened it.

"You asked for this." Karen said.

"I did." Asher noticed. "Look, this isn't the right time."

"Why not?"

"Something came up earlier that requires my current attention."

"Care to share it with me?"

"Not really. Possibly later."

Karen kept her calm, shaking her head slowly and only smiled toward Asher.

"Fair enough."

"Thank you." Asher nodded. "I will repay you in full."

Karen had walked to her car and Asher closed the door. Returning to the lair and he suited up. He contacted Jarvis on his travels to Henderson and while doing so, Karen was sitting in her car outside, to where she saw a Q-Arrow riding on a motorcycle not far from Asher's home.

"What in the hell?" She questioned.

Karen had started the ignition and followed in Q-Arrow's

direction. Jarvis had returned to the lair and kept the comms open to speak with Asher.

"I'm at the lair."

"Good." Asher said. "I'm on my way to Henderson now."

"Got it. Also, that young man you told me about. He was at the facility moments after you left."

"What did you say to him?"

"What would you expect?"

"He's following my trail, isn't he?" Asher laughed.

"He's not like most young men I've encountered. There's something older about him I can't yet understand."

"His mind hasn't been tainted, Jarvis. Plus, he's matured faster than most in this generation."

"Damn right, he did. It shows in his speech. His posture is one like ours."

"I'll see how he operates in the open. That'll determine his course."

"Understood."

Q-Arrow entered Henderson as dusk settled in. finding the city scattered with its civilians. They all shouted about a tree-like creature causing harm. They even made mention of it approaching the lake. Asher knew what lake.

"He's going toward Lake Las Vegas."

"Must be something there he's interested in."

"I'll find out."

Q-Arrow moved forward with Karen on his tail. She saw the commotion of the people in the streets. The fear in their voices and their eyes caused even the slightly notion of fear to touch her. Zooming behind her was Nero on a motorcycle. He sped past her.

"Another one?" She questioned.

Q-Arrow had reached Lake Las Vegas and what he saw was four figures. One of them taller than the three. He rose up from his bike and stood before them. Aiming four arrows.

"Turn around and face me."

They turned, Q-Arrow recognized three of them. The same Trio from the lab incident. Yet, the fourth one he hadn't encountered. It was the tree-like creature from the facility. Up close, the tree figure appeared to be human with rough brown bark covering its body. Leaves on its head, hands, and feet.

"Who and what are you?" Q-Arrow asked.

"I was known as Sam Weyman in my human form. Now, the humans have preferred to call me the Woodstalker."

"What do you want?"

"Change. You've seen the rising figures across the world. They're all being heroes. While, I choose to be their adversary."

"What for?"

"For pleasure and for a better life."

The Trio laughed and stepped up toward Q-Arrow and from around him came the roaring of a motorcycle. They turned and looked, seeing the arriving Nero. Geared up in his ninja-esque gear.

"A friend said you'll be here." Nero said.

"Noted." Q-Arrow nodded.

"You have a partner." Woodstalker said. "Good. More to kill

for our sake."

"Only ones failing this night are the four of you." Q-Arrow said aiming the arrows with Nero standing by his side. Prepared for the fight.

IV

ARROWHEAD

Q-Arrow and Nero faced the Trio and Woodstalker near the water of Lake Las Vegas. The opposing teams stared each other down. Their feet stepping against the dirt and their bodies still. Q-Arrow held the arrows in place. Nero was prepared to jump toward them. The trio spread themselves around to have a quicker gain and Woodstalker had already summoned branches from the ground beneath them.

"Make your move." Q-Arrow demanded. "We're not going anywhere."

In the distance behind them, Karen parked her car and stood outside, watching them prepare to fight near the lake.

"This is really happening."

Woodstalker stretched forth his arms, the ground had begun to shake and from the ground arose whipped thorns. Firing toward the two heroes. Q-Arrow fired the arrows and Nero flipped from the incoming whips. The arrows were dodged by Woodstalker and the Trio managed to move out of its way.

"Trio, take them down."

"With pleasure." Stampede said.

Q-Arrow fired several arrows toward the whips, ripping through them. He stood next to Nero as they saw the Trio incoming.

"Can you handle them on your own?" Q-Arrow asked.

"I've done it before haven't I."

Q-Arrow fired smoke arrows toward the ground in front of the Trio. From there, Nero moved swiftly through the smoke as Q-Arrow made his way toward Woodstalker. The trees around the lake started to quake as Q-Arrow stepped forward.

"What is it you truly want?"

"Power." Woodstalker said. "Power of the earth. The air. The sea. I want it all in my hands."

"You're not going to achieve it by these means."

"We'll find out."

Woodstalker rammed toward Q-Arrow, who started firing ice arrows. Attempting to freeze the hybrid one. Nero continued fighting against the Trio near the water of the lake. He was too fast for them. His quick movements confused them. Turning them around in circles. Their size gave them a disadvantage against someone as lean as Nero.

"What do we do!" Smasher questioned. "We need something fast!"

Nero arose from their feet and kicked Smasher in the chin and tripped him to the ground. Smasher fell as his two partners had watched. They turned to one another and saw Nero staring at them. Gesturing them to come and fight.

"He's toying around with us!" Stampede yelled. "We have to keep focus!"

"I have something in mind." Demolition gestured.

Nero went for them with his fist and Demolition ran toward Nero, grabbing him by his hair and tossed him into the lake. Stampede grinned and followed Demolition to the lake. Nero arose from the water only to be shoved underneath by Demolition.

"I like your idea, brother."

"I figured you would."

Nero fought his way to raise his head from the water only to receive a head butt from Demolition and a stomp from Stampede. The two together held Nero under the water. Q-Arrow was continuing to fire a variety of arrows toward Woodstalker who was lunging at him across the lake. Q-Arrow turned around and saw stampede and Demolition in the water. He looked around for Nero, only to turn back to the duo of the trio.

"Oh no." Q-Arrow said.

He ran for the duo with a different arrow in the bow. He fired the arrow and it hit the ground behind the duo, causing a great explosion. The duo flew across the ground and Nero rose up from the lake. Breathing hard.

"You're alright?!" Q-Arrow asked.

"I am now." Nero breathed. "What kind of arrow was that?"

"One that saved your life."

Nero nodded. They turned around toward Woodstalker. The exploding arrow knocked Stampede and Demolition out.

"It's just us now." Q-Arrow said. "Two against one."

"Unfair as it appears to be, I will overcome."

"Let's get this over with." Nero said. "I'm getting tired of this already."

Woodstalker lunged toward the two heroes. Q-Arrow equipped three arrows with firing starting to form on the heads. Nero dug into his pocket and pulled out a shuriken. Woodstalker arose two trees and Q-Arrow fired the arrows, burning the trees with Nero throwing the shuriken toward Woodstalker. Hitting him in his eye, he fell into the dirt. Q-Arrow fired another arrow toward Woodstalker and from the arrow bolted out a net. A net made of titanium fibers. Woodstalker was trapped.

"It's over?" Nero asked.

"I guess." Q-Arrow replied. "No telling."

Q-Arrow contacted Jarvis, telling him to call the police to gather Woodstalker. The police were on their way as Q-Arrow and Nero disappeared from the lake. Karen had watched the whole fight. She saw everything and even heard Q-Arrow speaking with Jarvis. She was certain of her possible thoughts. She returned to her home. The following days, the newspaper articles featured the headline title, *"The Q-Arrow Strikes Again."*, Woodstalker was placed in a secure facility. Nero had officially become part of the group with Asher giving him the codename, Shadow Hardy. Arwin Reese came to Las Vegas to work with Asher on several projects that pertain to the Q-Arrow's arsenal. Also, the Hitman had escaped prison and was on the watch list for the city.

Some days later after doing a search for the Hitman's possible whereabouts, Asher had arrived at one of his casinos and from behind he was greeted by Kenari Clark.

"Asher Dale." Kenari said.

Asher turned around, seeing Kenari. He smiled at him and

hugged him. Like brothers to one another.

"Kenari Clark! It is a pleasure to see you here."

"Likewise. I need to have a word with you in private. If you don't mind."

"Sure. Let's talk in the office."

I

<u>HARNESSING POWER</u>

Donald Fortune made his return to civilization after his seclusion in Nepal to refresh himself and to grow more in the mystic arts. Making his return, Fortune sensed a strange aura in the air. Particularly of the western world. He had begun to hear of terseness of the rising heroes. Before his seclusion, there was no talk of heroes existing unless people were speaking of historical tales and folklore pertaining to many cultures.

Fortune had reached more information of the heroes and learned of the ones that have been sighted in the States. Fortune read up on them and was left unimpressed. Therefore, Fortune had made it to his home, known to society as the Fortune Estate. Yet, to those of the mystical world, the Citadel of Enchantment. Fortune had entered and immediately, he was greeted by the benevolent energy of the Citadel.

"Feels better to have returned." Fortune said.

Fortune made his way toward his study and began reading up

on his books. Studying the grimoire, *The Book of Durriken*. Fortune spent a few days within his Citadel before ever walking out into society. Fortune's preference on the modern world was of one who's lost its morality and its declining state. Fortune didn't even dare to make an attempt at helping those outside his walls. Believing to be only wasting precious time.

During an afternoon, three days after Fortune's return, a knock came from the Citadel door. Fortune stepped out of his study, steady as he approached the door. He wasn't sure who could be visiting him at these hours unless they were someone he knew and was close to. Fortune opened the door and standing outside was a young man. In his twenties.

"Who might you be?" Fortune asked.

"My name is Thomas Bradley. I've come to speak with Donald Fortune."

"Well, you're looking at him. What can I do for you? My offices aren't open right now. As you see, I've just returned from a long trip."

"From Nepal." Thomas said.

"How do you know?"

"I know your reason for leaving civilization. I'm not a noisy person. But, I've read up on your work in the mystic arts. That is why I'm here."

"You want me to assist you in the mystic arts?"

"I want you to train me. Train me so I can become as great of a master as you."

"Young man, are you aware of the things you're getting yourself into? The supernatural realm isn't one of easy pickings. It's one of many trials, tribulations, and tests. Each will arise from random circumstances. Why bother with it?"

"Because this world is falling, and it will come to an end soon. I can sense it."

"The decline and the immorality, huh?"

"It's growing. Faster than what most have predicted. Please, teach me of the mystic arts and maybe I can attempt to save my people."

"Your people?"

"I'm native to New Orleans."

"Ah. You've delved in the voodoo arts before haven't you?"

"Just once. It's not compared to what I've heard what you can do."

Fortune nodded and widen open the door. Gesturing Thomas to enter and he did. Fortune shut the door.

Over in Centro of the Kingdom of Judgedath, it's leader primarily known as the Sinister Judge watched Fortune and Thomas speak in the Citadel through a invisible, yet, powerful portal in his throne room. he could hear everything they were saying, even the details of Fortune's time in Nepal of casting out demons from a woman. the cloaked and hooded king was visited in his throne room by his soldiers called the Judgedroids. Visual replicas of the Judge himself.

"Everything is ready, my master."

"Excellent." Judge said. "Send them out at once."

"Yes, my lord." The Judgedroid left the throne room.

Judge watched the Judgedroid exit the room and he returned his gaze back toward the portal. Only his glowing blue eyes could be seen from the shadow of the hood. Judge stood up from his throne and stepped down to the center of the room. Upon his crest.

"I now must pay my old adversary a visit."

Judge twirled his hands and the crest had warped into a wormhole. The hole creating its own wind, blowing through the room and Judge's cloak flowing with the violet shining from his suit. Judge dove himself into the portal and it was gone. Nothing but silence was left in the throne room.

II

<u>HOMEFRONT</u>

Thomas gazed at the sight of the Citadel of Enchantment. Fortune stopped in is steps and spotted how the Citadel was an astounding object toward the young man. Fortune gently smiled.

"Don't get too attached just yet." Fortune said. "Follow me, Thomas."

Thomas followed Fortune to his study. When Thomas entered the study, he was amazed at the number of books and scrolls laid on the shelves against the walls. He walked around them, touching the spines of the books.

"Are all of these grimoires?"

"You could say that. Some however, are just standard books. Few at least are maps."

"What kind of maps?"

"Ones that are useful to a mystic artist."

Fortune grabbed the book on his desk and handed to Thomas. Just to have a quick look. Thomas had his look and Fortune closed the book. Thomas was confused as Fortune sat down at the desk.

"Sit down." Fortune said.

Thomas sat down, and Fortune nodded.

"You need to tell me why you want to get involved in this field."

"Because I want to make a change to the world."

"I understand that. But, there are other things in this field that are more prone to things outside of this world."

"The supernatural can help heal this world."

"That it can. Yet, it will not."

"Why not?" Thomas wondered. "How many of you are there in the world today? I'm sure you can't be the only one."

"There are others. Handling their business as usual. Business that keeps this earth safe from the malevolent forces who claw their way to get in."

"So, it's all real. The demons. The malevolent forces. All of it."

"It is. You can add angels into the mix as well. I haven't seen one since I began my training."

"I read the Mystic Father trained you."

"That he did."

"How was it? Learning from someone of that much power?"

"Tempting and terrifying." Fortune said. "Many profess to enter this field only to leave it either with a broken spirit or in a casket."

"Broken spirit?"

"They didn't have the stomach to handle the darker situations. The tough choices we all must make when they're staked up against us."

"I can take them." Thomas said. "I have faith. I can and I will."

Fortune nodded while studying Thomas' body language. "So you say."

More knocking came from the front door. Fortune turned his head and sighed. Thomas only wondered who else was coming to visit the powerful Doctor Fortune. Fortune stood up from the desk and went to answer the door. Thomas stood up and watched as Fortune opened the door and standing there was one of Fortune's closest allies.

"Huang." Fortune said.

"I heard you returned to society." Huang said. "Better that I come to visit you."

"And you have."

Fortune and Huang hugged. Close as brothers in the mystic arts. Both happy to see one another. Thomas watched and was learning of a kinder side to Fortune.

"How was Nepal?"

"It was useful. I had the time to strength my connection to the mystic realm and I've never felt better. Although, I had to deal with some demons while I was there."

"How many?"

"Few enough to easily cast away."

"Did they follow you to Nepal? Were they sent by one of our enemies?"

"No. a young woman was possessed with them. I helped her

from her pain."

"The usual service of our kind."

"Always."

Huang walked with Fortune and he spotted Thomas standing by the door of the study.

"Who's the young man?"

"Thomas Bradley. He came to the door before you did. Said he wants to learn what I know."

"He wants to enter this field? Of all things?"

"I said the same. Yet, he's persistent. He wants to help change the world for the better."

Huang walked toward Thomas and stood before him. Measuring him and sensing his mystical strength from within. Searching his aura.

"His aura is strong, Fortune."

"I felt it." Fortune added. "He has some potential. I just need to see him in action."

"When can we do that?" Thomas asked.

"When the situation calls for it." Huang said. "Better to present it in a battle besides regular training."

"You and I both know there is no regular training in this field." Fortune said. "We learned how to do this when our enemies came upon us."

"True. We learned fast and steady."

"Made us strong."

Thomas caught something from the corner of his eyes. It looked like a shadow. Glowing with little light by the front door while Fortune and Huang talked. Thomas moved closer and could see silhouettes standing outside.

"Doctor." Thomas said. "Someone's outside."

"Not possible." Huang said. "There was no one behind me for miles."

"Maybe they're not invited." Fortune said. "Prepare yourselves."

The door burst open and from the debris enter Judgedroids. Firing energy blasts toward the three men. Fortune moved across the room, levitating above the ground. Huang twirled his hands and formed mystical gauntlets. Thomas was confused and only followed what the two mystic artists were doing.

"Thomas. Stay back." Fortune said. "Let us handle this."

"What are they?" Huang asked.

"I've seen their schematics once." Fortune said. "Back in Centro. In Judgedath."

"Ah." Huang added. "They're his."

"Yes. They are."

Fortune fired blasts of energy at the moving droids. Hitting them with every hit. Huang ran toward a few and pummeled them with the increased strength of the gauntlets. Thomas could only watch. He was amazed at Fortune and Huang's impressive movement and mystic arts.

"There's only ten of them." Fortune said. "This will be over soon."

Fortune swiped his hand, creating a sharp wave of energy. Glowing as blue as water. The wave collided with the Judgedroids, ripping them in half. The machines fell to the floor and Fortune made his way down to the ground.

"Least it wasn't as tough."

"They're only robots, Huang. These were only the fodder. I'm expecting the arsenal soon enough."

"You would expect the firepower."

"It's what he's known for. Showing off what he possesses."

Fortune stood over the remains of the Judgedroids.

"He's coming."

"Who's coming?" Thomas asked.

"The one who sent them."

"If that's the case, Fortune, we must prepare this Citadel. We must gear up at once."

"We will." Fortune said. "Right now, we need to learn why he chose to attack us now."

"You know the man better than I do."

"I do. We were friends once. Long ago. It's funny and true. Sometimes friends always take the opposite side and become enemies."

Fortune turned to Thomas and approached him.

"You'll have to aid us in facing Sinister Judge."

"Sinister Judge? The ruler of Centro?"

"You've heard of him?" Huang asked. "How?"

"His rule signals across the world. He keeps the other countries at bay from invading his own. He doesn't even attend the UN meetings."

"Judge has his own ways of doing things." Fortune said.

"Which is why I need to confront him."

Making their way back to the study, they could feel a tremor coming from the ground around the Citadel. Fortune took a look outside and what he saw was an army. Larger than the Judgedroids and they weren't machines. Huang also saw them as did Thomas.

"What are those?" Thomas asked.

"The dark forces." Huang said.

"Judge summoned them." Fortune said. "He's preparing an invasion upon us."

They looked out at the incoming horde of the Moronic Ones. Dimensional beings who are consumed with the malevolent energies of the mystic realms.

III

<u>HOMESTEAD</u>

"What should we do, Fortune?" Huang questioned.

"This is my home." Fortune replied. "I'm not going anywhere."

"So, we're going to hold this place?' Thomas wondered.

"Exactly."

Fortune raised his hands above his head and from them warped shields designed in emblems of the mystic arts. Triangles, hexagons, circles, and shapes unknown to society. From them, Fortune fired an arsenal of energy beams toward the Moronic Ones standing outside of the Citadel. The blasts caused the dimensional beings to take several steps back. They circled the Citadel.

"What are they doing?" Thomas said.

"Coming up with a strategy of their own." Fortune said. "That's how wicked they are."

The Moronic Ones continued their devising and over in the distance from the Citadel, Sinister Judge stood. Overseeing the event and his eyes kept their gaze on the Citadel.

"I have an idea."

"What kind of idea, Thomas?" Fortune asked.

"Let them in."

"Why would we allow that to happen?" Huang asked. "You want to die today?"

"No. Open the door and once they enter, we can annihilate them all at once."

"I don't think that's possible."

"Not if we do it alone." Fortune added.

"What are you suggesting?"

"We combine our power. Fuse it into one. With that much power, it can remove these beings from the land."

Huang looked over to Thomas and nodded his head slightly. Thomas smiled.

"Release your power into this mark on the floor."

Fortune twirled his hands and from the floor burned a mark. A mark made of a hexagon and three circles intertwined with one larger circle.

"I see." Huang said.

The mark was ready and the three moved their mystic powers into the mark. It grew, and the color of the mark brightened. It gave off the stench of burning metal and from it arose a bright beam. The beam bolted through the Citadel and into the sky, causing the Moronic Ones to pause in their steps. Sinister Judge could see the beam from his distance.

"They've opened it." Judge remarked.

From the beam exited an entity. Fortune saw the entity and immediately bowed his face to the floor as did Huang. Thomas, unaware of what's happening stood frozen as he saw the entity coming out of the beam. The entity was dressed in a white robe and its face glowed like the brightness of a quenching flame. His countenance was of an old man, yet, he appeared young in his feats.

"Mystic Father." Fortune said. "I wasn't aware you would appear."

"I have for a good cause. One that requires the vanishing of these creatures."

The Mystic Father waved his hand toward the window and from his might, the Moronic Ones were wiped out. Gone. Judge saw the beings vanish from the golden wave that came from the Citadel.

"He brought you out." Judge said. "This is more than I anticipated."

Judge turned around as a one-dimensional portal opened behind him. He walked through it and was gone.

Fortune stood up and gazed outside, seeing the Moronic Ones have left. Huang and Thomas noticed the quietness of the outside as they stood around the Mystic Father. Fortune and Huang trembled, Thomas was left confused. He didn't know what to make of the tall figure standing before him and why Fortune and Huang were terrified at its presence.

"Why have you come, Mystic Father?" Fortune asked.

"I've come to give you the clear details of all this commotion."

"You know what's happening?"

"Sinister Judge released the Moronic Ones onto your land to tarp you in this place. Unfortunately, Judge may have forgotten my sense of the world and its goings. When you were fusing your power together, I used it as a means of entry. My help was necessary to speak to the three of you concerning what's about to come."

"What's coming?" Thomas asked.

"It concerns you all and your futures."

"What's coming this way, Father?" Fortune wondered.

"Darkness. Pure darkness." The Mystic Father declared. "A darkness that hasn't been seen in this world since the time of Harold Vosloo."

"Harold Vosloo?" Huang said. "The one who constructed the Life Artifact."

"The Holy Artifact of Life as its been called." Fortune said. "Why it is a concern now?"

"I know you're now aware of its whereabouts. How it was taken and used in the Battle of Retropolis."

"I read up on the event." Fortune said. "It didn't say anything about that artifact being used to start it."

"The artifact's return has summoned most of the dark forces in the universe and they're on their way to this world to claim it. To open it up and release the dark god that remains inside its prison."

"Is Judge a part of this?"

"His part is only a small matter in its beginning."

"It seems so." Huang said. "We know of Judge's motives."

"Judge is only out to gain whatever it is he desires for himself. The artifact would only bring much pain and sorrow if it were to end up in his hands."

"Where is Judge now?"

"In his country of Centro. He was here and left after I eliminated the Moronic Ones."

"I have an idea, Father." Fortune said.

"I already know. He's expecting you to show up."

Huang approached Fortune and nodded as they looked toward the Mystic Father. Thomas was left confused once more. Feeling somewhat out of place. He didn't expect his visitation to receive this much detail. Yet, he was learning.

"Father, myself and Fortune will travel to Centro and confront Judge on his stead."

"As you shall. But, take Thomas with you. He will need the experience of confronting a powerful adversary such as Judge."

"You know what will become of him after this." Fortune said. "This is all part of his future isn't it?"

"He is destined to become a powerful user in the mystic arts. Someday, he will claim your title of Supreme Enchanter. Until then, you must train him in the arts."

"I will do so." Fortune nodded.

"I will be there with you. Remember."

The Mystic Father had vanished through a similar beam through the mark. Thomas approached Fortune and Huang concerning the Father's words for his future. Fortune nodded toward him as did Huang.

"You heard him. We have some traveling to do."

"Do you own a plane?" Thomas asked.

"We're not taking the usual transportation to get to Centro."

"Then, how will we get there?"

Fortune flicked his hand and conjured an inter-dimensional portal. He turned to Thomas. It appeared similar to Judge's only with a change of color. Judge's was a dark blue and Fortune's is a dark violet.

"Like so."

"Nice." Thomas smiled.

"Best we get going, Fortune."

Fortune nodded and the three walked through the portal and it closed. On the other side, it opened, revealing a large castle standing before them. The sky gray with dark clouds. The sounds of machines could be heard from miles. The atmosphere itself was dark and it trembled Thomas.

"He senses it." Huang noticed.

"As do we." Fortune said. "Welcome to Judgedath, Centro."

They stood looking out toward Palace Judge. The residence of Sinister Judge.

IV

<u>THE JUDGMENT OF FORTUNES</u>

Fortune, Huang, and Thomas set their feet upon the stairs of Palace Judge. They moved with ease, noticing many of the Judgedroids moving on throughout the area.

"What do we do about them?" Thomas asked.

"We're here for Judge. Nothing else." Fortune said.

The three make their way up the stairs and as they step onto the final stair, the palace doors open. The opening of the doors releases a gust of air toward them to where they had to raise their arms to keep their balance. After the gust had calmed, they entered the palace. Fortune knew Judge was aware of their presence and given them entry. No other option could be possible. Otherwise, the Judgedroids would've killed them on the spot.

Inside, Fortune saw Judge sitting in the seat of his throne. The palace doors shut with a clicking tick. Thomas was uncertain of their lives as was Huang. Fortune stepped forward facing the ruler of Centro.

"Welcome to Judgedath, Fortune." Judge said.

"You knew I would come after what you sent to my home."

"And it worked as planned."

"Why did you do it?"

"Because of your uncertain return to civilization. You should've stayed in your solitude. Nepal fitted you best. Not the Western world."

"How would you know what works best for me?"

"We were once allies in the mystic arts. Only, until you weren't strong enough to take the measure of the otherworldly and the powers it could've granted you. You could've been a god to this world and instead, you've chosen to be a hero. Like the others."

"I am not a hero." Fortune declared. "I am only helping those in need of supernatural harm. I'm just a scattered soul doing a bit of good."

"Scattered is one way of putting it. Saving a strange woman in Nepal from demons. Now, you're recruiting young men into your fold. Are you positive Thomas is able to stand amongst you and Huang in the face of danger?"

"He's here now. Standing before you."

"Maybe so." Judge nodded, raising up from his throne. "But, the three of you aren't powerful enough to defeat me. I am the Sinister Judge and you have stepped foot in my palace within the borders of my city and my country. There is no other ruler in this land but Judge and Judge will remain forever sovereign."

Judge walked down to the floor. Standing before the three. He circled them as they banded together. Their eyes locked on Judge's movements.

"Don't tremble yet." Judge said. "You can have that pleasure once you're done here."

"You mean once we're dead and our bodies burned."

"To a degree. Judge always gets what he wants and what I desire now is for the three of you to die by my hand. That way you will always know Judge is a just ruler."

Fortune raised his hands as they glowed a shining red. Huang also stances himself while Thomas followed Fortune's suit. Judge had studied them. He was savoring the first attack.

"Good."

Judge smashed his fist into the floor, causing a tremor which knocked the three off their feet. Fortune turned around and Judge was in the air, coming to crash upon him with his foot. Fortune teleported to the opposite area of the throne room as Judge crashed onto the floor. The armor of Judge shook, and Judge turned to him as he deflected the blast fired at him by Huang and Thomas.

"How can you be the Supreme Enchanter and not Judge?"

"I have the willpower. You only have the force."

Fortune summoned a hole and Judge stepped through the hole.

"How?"

"You could've learned this when we were allies. Instead you denied such power."

Judge fired a bolt of mystic energy, hitting Fortune in the chest and he bounced off the wall from the force. Fortune laid face first on the ground and Judge turned his attention toward Huang and Thomas.

"Keep doing what you're doing!" Huang told Thomas.

"I'm trying my best."

"I am aware you're young, Thomas. You just found the wrong mentor. Judge is the perfect mentor."

"I've found the right mentor and his name is Doctor Fortune."

"How sad of you." Judge said before knocking Thomas to the floor with a wave of energy from his hand.

Judge swiftly moved over and snatched Huang by his throat and held him up. Fortune, moving groggy looked and saw Huang in the air. He looked over and saw Thomas on the floor.

"This is not right." Fortune said.

"It is only fitting that one of you will become the ash to my flames for the night." Judge said to Huang. "It appears you will be the one to heat up Judge's throne."

"Not likely." Huang said.

Fortune stood up and stared at Judge. He twirled his hands and held them out. All his fingers stood except his ring fingers and his index fingers. His eyes were closed. His energy was keen toward Judge.

"*Mehabta. Senuta. Shawmeera. Et. Intuckna.*" Fortune chanted. "*Paberna. Detomo. Sovena. Ut. Hamhor!*"

The air around the throne room had exploded and Judge

tossed Huang against the wall next to Thomas and turned toward Fortune.

"What have you transpired this time?" Judge asked.

"A little aid for the moment." Fortune smiled.

In between them was a breaching of the realms. A tear was created and from the tear arose the Mystic Father. He stood in between Fortune and Judge.

"You came." Fortune said.

"Why have you trespassed?!" Judge yelled. "You are standing in the throne room of the Sinister Judge."

"I know where I stand. You do not."

"Judge must be stopped!" Fortune said.

"Not on this day." Mystic Father said.

"What?"

"There are plans for Judge. It is not his time."

"I do as I choose." Judge said. "And I answer to no one. Not even a god."

The Mystic Father stood toward Judge and the ruler of Centro didn't back down. The Mystic Father could feel the power within Judge and it was strong and it was malevolent. The Mystic Father nodded and turned to Fortune.

"This battle will be cut short. Saved for a later date."

What are you going to do?"

"I will return you and your allies back to the Citadel. Judge will remain here until the proper time has called."

The Mystic Father created another portal and Fortune, Huang, and Thomas walked through it.

"Don't take this interruption lightly." Judge said. "There will come a time where you won't be there to save your Supreme Enchanter, Mystic one."

"History will provide the tale. Prophecy has already settled the story."

The Mystic Father vanished through his own portal. Judge remained the sole one in the throne room. He walked atop the stairs and sat back in his seat. He sighed. Not of distress, but of victory

Fortune, Huang, and Thomas had returned to the Citadel. Fixing up whatever was damaged by the Moronic Ones' invasion.

"What are you going to do about the boy?" Huang asked.

"He's seen our world with his own eyes. However, few it may be. He'll remain with us. I'll train him in the mystic arts."

Huang nodded and return to his work. Fortune called Thomas to his study and there he began to teach him of the mystic arts. Back in Centro, Judge was studying a map. The map was detailed with the northernmost part of North America in its sights. A Judgedroid entered the war room.

"Everything is prepared, my lord."

"Good." Judge said. Slamming his fist onto the map and once he removed it, he stares at the name of the country. Canada.

KULAR THE AQUA-BARBARIAN: SAGA OF THE AQUA-BARBARIAN

I

<u>RISEN FROM THE SEA</u>

From the ocean, Kular arose and made his way toward the land. Seeing it ahead and he made way for it. Nearing it, he found humans laying on the sands of the shore. Confusing to him for a moment, but, a unsettling scene for those on the shore. Kular walked out of the sea, wearing his battle armor and carrying his trident. His presence caused a few of the humans to remove themselves from the shore. Seeking a place to hide from the risen Atlantean.

In Kular's mind was a replay of the *Battle of the Kings* and his love for his wife Kara and his kingdom of Atlantis. However, the Aqua-Barbarian was keen to meet the rising heroes he's heard about for some time and nothing would stop him from accomplishing his goal on the land. Kular walked off the shore and into the grassy field where others were sitting. Dressed in beach shorts and sandals by their vehicles barbequing. Having a casual fellowship amongst people. They turned and stared at Kular.

"No costume party here, my boy."

"Where are these rising heroes?" Kular asked. "I demand to speak with them."

"You won't find any here." The beachgoer replied. "We haven't seen any."

"Where could I find them?"

"They're all over the world, man. Don't you watch the news?"

Kular glanced around the area. Scouting the surroundings and from the distance, he could see tall buildings. Their lights somewhat dim from his point of view.

"This land. What is its name?"

"What?"

"The name of this land. What is it?"

"America."

"North or South?" Kular asked.

"North America. You're standing in North America on United States soil."

"And the name of the neighboring city?"

"It's called Miami."

"Miami." Kular nodded. "Thank you for your assistance. I will take this matter into my own hands."

Kular removed himself from their sight and left the beach. Making his goal to finding the rising heroes closer than before.

II

ATLANTEAN MEETS NUBREED

Traveling through the southeast of the United States, Kular went from Miami to Atlanta to Nashville. His motives were still intact as he demanded to meet with the rising heroes. Everywhere he went, no one of the residents could tell him where they may be. Irrigated by humanity's emotion of fearing the unknown, Kular had found himself entering the bay of the city of Chicago.

When he arose from the bay, his eyes had a sight of the rising heroes. Kular found himself witnessing a battle between the Yonderers and their adversary General Rilla. Rilla was taking down the Yonderers in their novice age of fighting. Kular jumped from the bay onto the streets between the opposing forces.

"Who is this?" Rilla asked. "An unknown ally of your side?"

"I don't know who he is." Valinor said. "No idea."

"I am Kular, King of Atlantis."

"Atlantis." Rilla said. "How interesting."

"He's somewhat like me." The Surf uttered.

"Don't get egotistical on us." Gale replied.

"I have come to speak with the rising heroes."

"Why the heroes, Atlantean King?" Rilla asked. "What is the purpose of this visit?"

"To see what the surface world has to offer."

"I'm intrigued."

Rilla raised his arms, shoving the Yonderers across from himself and Kular. Valinor fought against the wave of Rilla's power and rushed toward him with his staff. Valinor twisted the staff and swiped it across Rilla's chest. The impact of the attack knocked Rilla to the pavement while Kular continued to watch on. Emerald and Crystalax teamed up on Rilla while Gale and Magic Carpet kept his power at bay. Rilla was weakening from the combined force of the Yonderers. Eventually, Rulla succumbed to the attacks and passed out. After the fight, Lois Frost confronted Kular.

"Who are you again?" She wondered. "Just for clarity's sake."

"I am Kular, the King of Atlantis."

"And why are you here in Chicago?"

"To see those such as yourselves. The humans call you the rising heroes."

"Heroes?" Lois gestured.

"Yes." Kular said. "I've heard about your kind throughout the mouths of my enemies."

"Oh." Valinor scoffed. "You're talking about the other guys. We're not exactly heroes around here. Most of the time we're the ones attacked and ridiculed. Only because we can do things average humans cannot. We have power. Some limited. Others untapped."

Rilla had started to awaken, seeing Kular speaking with the Yonderers. He arose from the ground and flew toward them. Kular caught him coming in the corner of his eye and snatched Rilla from the air and slammed him into the road. The Yonderers were impressed by Kular's superhuman strength as was Rilla.

"You could help us." Emerald gestured.

"No thanks. I have my own priorities to concern with."

Kular turned and walked away from the young team.

"Will we meet again?" Valinor asked. "just on better terms?"

Kular stopped and turned, "When the time calls for it."

Kular continue walking and returned to the bay, dwelling under the water and vanishing from the sight of the Yonderers. The Yonderers went to apprehend Rilla, but he was gone.

"Shit." Valinor said.

"Another day, Valinor." Lois mentioned. "He'll come back around."

"And more than likely not alone."

III

<u>CHAMPIONS</u>

Kular continued his traveling and found himself now in the regions of the north. The temperature had dropped, snow settled on the ground. Kular arose from the frozen waters, discovering he had reached an entry point into a forest. Kular walked on the shoreline of the water to the land. Keeping a single track and forming a perimeter only he would comprehend.

Continuing his walk, Kular heard rustling in the forest and held his stance. Ready to fight if necessary. The rustling increased and before Kular could take a step closer, the Champions had emerged from the forest. They paused seeing Kular standing in front of them. Behind the Champions appeared their leader, Commander Norland. Kular measured the Commander and he done the same. Kular was impressed by Norland's uniform. Noticing the armor plates set in the areas of the suit.

"You're not from around, are you?" Norland asked.

"Who are you, stranger?" Kular asked in return.

"Commander Norland. The defender of the nation of Canada.

And the world at most. You?"

"I am Kular the Aqua-Barbarian. King of Atlantis."

Atlantis is something Norland has never heard of existing. He's only been told the myths and legends of the underwater city. Now, he's standing face to face with the ruler of that city. Norland immediately shows Kular respect in his role as king. Kular sensed the respect flowing from Norland. He glanced over to the Champions and they stood guard. Ready for a fight if necessary.

"Then, what brings you up to Canada?"

"I have been searching for these rising heroes I've heard much about."

"Rising heroes." Norland said. "Why do you wish to see them?"

"Are you one of them?"

"I've been called one a few times in my service."

"Then, I require your aid."

"My aid?"

"There are forces in the deep who are rising up to do battle. To make war with my kingdom. I desire to have a few of these rising heroes to accompany me into the war and to save my kingdom."

Norland approached Kular. Both men stood toe to toe. Equal height. Kular was much bigger than Norland when it came to muscular structure. Norland's Champions: Canadian Hawk, Steve Nixon, and Whiplash were unsettled by the presence of the Aqua-Barbarian. The surroundings quiet with only a slight whistle of the chilly wind.

"I would help you." Norland said. "Really, I would. But, there are matters taking place in my country that require my services. As do my team."

"I understand your words, Commander Norland."

Kular walked toward the water. Norland and the Champions watched him as he stepped into the water, reaching his waist. He turned back toward them.

"I am sure when the time does occur, you will aid me. As I would do the same."

Norland nodded with respect. "I'll keep that in mind, King Kular."

Kular nodded and submerged himself into the water.

"What are we going to tell Nader about him?" Nixon asked.

"I figure Nader already knows about him and Atlantis."

"We could ask him you know." Canadian Hawk suggested. "Just to see what he says."

"Another time." Norland said. "Right now, we have a mission to complete."

Norland and the Champions returned to the forest to continue their mission.

IV

A SPECTER'S CONCLUSION

Moving onward, Kular continued searching the world for the rising heroes. Nearing another nightfall, Kular took the time to rest. In preparation, a bright white light emerged out of the air in front of him with the sound of a great boom equal to a meteor breaking through the atmosphere of the heavens. Kular stood tall and was ready to fight. From the light appeared a figure cloaked in all white with a black helmet underneath its white hood.

"Who are you?" Kular asked.

"I am one of many paths. The generations of Man call me the Specter Errant."

"And why have you come to me?"

"Kular of Atlantis. You have chosen a journey that will only send you back to your kingdom empty and lost."

"How so?"

"This quest of yours to discover the heroes roaming the world will not only end you up at Atlantis, you'll start a war between yourself and the kingdoms of the seas."

"How can I know you're telling me the truth?"

"I see everything. I hear everything. I know everything. From your birth to your death. To the battles and to the wars. I have foreseen your future and I am warning you, this meeting with the heroes of Earth will only increase the wars of your life."

"What are you proposing me to do?"

"Turn back now." Specter Errant demanded. "Return to your kingdom and be with your wife and your people. Live a life worth remembering when you reach your old age."

"What if war is what I crave? What if blood is what I desire?"

"Then, you will be granted as you crave and as your desire."

Kular approached the Errant. Feeling the beaming light on his rough skin. He looked into the Errant's eyes and could not see pupils. Only the shining white light within them.

"What are you?" Kular wondered. "Really."

"I am above your understanding, Aqua-Barbarian. I witnessed your encounter with the Yonderers and the Champions. Howbeit, they managed not to combat you on their territory. In which, they could have and more than likely, would've defeated you without your knowing."

Kular took in the Errant's words with gratitude.

"Tell me, what of my near future? Will Kaiser return to face me in another war? Or will there be a land-dweller who will seek to conquer my kingdom for themselves?"

"All of the above." The Errant declared. "You will face enemies sea and land alike. Monsters and aliens. Gods and heroes. Your future is filled with war. Some you will win and others you will lose. Battles you shall have and battles you shall lose."

"Do these rising heroes know of your existence?"

"Only a select few."

"Why?" Kular wondered. "Is that the way you work up here? It isn't like those of the sea."

"I work in ways beyond the comprehension of those in the sea and those of the land. My place is one of the other realms in existence. I travel through them all. It is my purpose."

"The others must learn of your kind to exist. Imagine how you can aid them in times of great distress."

"The remaining will learn of my presence in a short time."

The shining light busted behind the Errant, who was beginning to take his leave from Kular's resting spot. Before he left, Kular approached him closer.

"Will we meet again in the future?"

"You will find out." The Errant said.

Specter Errant disappeared through the shining light and only the darkness remained in the land. The moon kept her light on the ground, yet, it was not even equal to the light of the Specter Errant. Kular laid down on the ground atop the grass and slept.

V

ENEMIES AND ALLIES

Kular dreamt of a world where the sea-dwellers and the land-dwellers lived in a peaceful world. A world where neither side boasted of the higher gain to the other. The King of Atlantis wished for a world such as he dreamt the rising heroes would be in allegiance with him and they would overcome those who oppose the peaceful rule of the heroes.

"We will achieve our victory." Kular said in front of a massive and mixed crowd.

A crowd of heroes and civilians standing together. There was no anger amongst them toward one another. They were in unity. All spoke the same matters. However, their anger was targeted toward the evildoers of the world. Notably their names were known to Kular strangely to him how he's never met them. Their names were written on the walls of the Atlantean throne which sat above the seas for all the land-dwellers to see.

"Here are our targets." Kular noted to his armed soldiers. "We find each of them and we kill them. Simple as is."

Kular would go off with his army and the rising heroes would join him in taking out their enemy. A peaceful life Kular dreamt of, yet, he may never achieve such a world.

VI

<u>FROM THE LAND TO THE SEA</u>

Upon waking up from his dream of a perfect future, Kular sat and took in the surroundings. Never seeing much of the land before in his reign as king. Kular meditated on his visitants since appearing from the sea and stepping foot on land. From meeting those on the beach, to traveling across the country and confronting the Yonderers as they fought General Rilla. Kular's never seen such young warriors as them in decades. They amazed him, and their feats proved worthy of potential alliances in the future.

Taking himself further up north and meeting Commander Norland and his Champions. Intrigued by their style and motives, they revealed to Kular a different side of land-dwellers. One he hopes will prove useful in the ever-knowing need of a world war between the land and the sea. Which, such a future proved to be a near reality when he was visited by the Specter Errant, who forewarned him of his future. A future of wars and battles. Some he will win and others he will lose.

Now, Kular has set himself aside, ready to return to his kingdom to give the news to his wife and his people. Setting himself a course, Kular decided to move eastward, directing himself in a path toward the Atlantic Ocean. As Kular made his moves by walking. Never tiring nor sweating from the long amounts of travel, Kular found himself in the presence of another group of beings: The Unkinds.

VII

<u>TWO KINGS</u>

Kular stood still as he faced the Unkinds. They surrounded him, the Royal Elite- Ophiuchus, Cygnus, Aquila the Queen and Halo Lock the King. Kular stood his ground as Halo hovered down from the air toward him. Stepping foot onto the ground, faced toward Kular. Both kings were equal in height and their structure was near even.

"Who are you?" Halo asked. "What are you?"

"Best if I ask you the same." Kular replied. "Who are all of you? Sky-beings?"

"We come from another world. A world must more advanced, yet similar to yours. We are the Royal Elite. Meet Cygnus, Ophiuchus, Aquila my wife. I am Halo Lock. The King."

"Another king." Kular muttered.

"What is that meant to mean?"

"I am Kular the Aqua-Barbarian. King of the Seas. King of Atlantis and its surrounding borders."

"Atlantis? What is this place you speak of?"

"I dwell in the oceans of this world. Not indifferent than how you dwell in the skies."

"They are different. You are saying you live under the submergence. We live above the firmament."

"Yet, why are you here? On land?"

"I could ask you the same. I thought you said your kingdom was one of the seas. Not the land which we both stand on."

"I have business to attend to on this soil."

"As do we and you've managed to get in our way."

"Your way? You stepped in front of me."

"Don't raise your tone with me, Sea-King. I am a king of the Royal Elite. You are just a king of the liquids of this world."

"Don't undermine me because you come from the skies."

"That is all which should be said about our differences. We come from above. You come from beneath."

Kular and Halo locked eyes. Aquila ran in between the two kings. Pushing them from each other. Her hair blowing between them like a flag through the air.

"Beloved, don't fight."

"Why shouldn't I?"

"Because, we have more urgent concerns to deal with. Let this Sea-King go on about his business. As we should."

Beeping sounds emerge from the two members of the Elite. Halo and Aquila turn toward them. Cygnus stepped forward, holding a device in his hand. Like a Smartphone to humanity. On the device was a radar and it was spiking.

"He's near." Cygnus declared. "We need to move, my king."

Halo nodded. "Let's move."

The Elite hovered in the air and flew. Halo set himself to leave and turned back to Kular. Kular pointed at the King of the Unkinds. Fury was searing in his eyes.

"The next time we meet, your wife won't be standing between us."

"In time, we will know which king is the true king." Halo smiled before flying off.

Kular watched them in the air and returned to his business. Traveling on foot for many miles, never tiring out, Kular approached a small town named Mass City. He stopped for a quick rest. As he set his mind to continue moving south, Kular spotted a TV in one of the neighboring buildings. On the monitor was details of an unseen force moving through the city of Retropolis. Taking down criminals and leaving behind a mark detailed only with the letter "S" and a sword insignia.

"What is that?" Kular wondered.

"He's still out there." A man said drinking against the wall. "He can't be stopped."

"How come he can't be stopped?"

"He has a higher power watching over him. Everyone knows there's something to him with that sword."

He turned his sights toward the road and walked. People around him didn't bother him due to the fact they've seen many strange things occur in the area. Mainly between Mass City and Retropolis. Kular had set his mind, he's heading to Retropolis to learn more about his unseen force.

VIII

HALLOW GROUNDS

Kular had entered the city of Retropolis. Its gothic, yet, futuristic nature and complexion through him off. He walked down the roads, nearly being hit head-on by the vehicles. He looked around in the sky and near the top of the buildings. He was searching for the one he saw on the monitor and didn't find him. Kular had continued searching amongst the city as he could with his great speed and he couldn't find the one he was looking for. He turned over and saw near him a forest, the Retropolis Forest. Kular walked in and the shadows of the tress covered him. Moving through, he could hear rustling in the trees. Pausing himself and gazing the surroundings with his eyes.

"Who are you?" A voice said behind him.

Kular turned and faced the figure which spoke the words. The figure was cloaked in black and its eyes glowed white. Almost as white as shining snow.

"Who are you?" The figure asked again.

"I am Kular. King of Atlantis."

"Atlantis is pretty far from here isn't it?"

"That it is."

"Then, why are you here? In Retropolis?"

"To find the one I saw on the TV. The unseen force which drives evil away."

The cloaked figure walked into the moonlight on the ground and there, his presence was revealed unto Kular.

"I am the unseen force. I am The Swordman."

Kular measured The Swordman. Seeing the sword sheathed on his back, intertwined with the dark, black cloak he wore. His face was hidden by the dark gray mask and the black cloaked hood above it. Eclipsed in dark gray armor from neck to toe. The Swordman spoke with a deep voice, yet, not with a mumble, but with a stillness. One where everyone could understand his words when they were spoken.

"Why have you come to this place?" The Swordman asked.

"I have come to see what you can do. How you're able to cleanse this city of criminals. You're just one man."

"One man can accomplish many things if he sets his mind to it."

"And your mind is settled."

"Settled since I was crowned the Master Swordman of my Creed."

"The Creed of Swords you speak of?"

"It's spoken of in Atlantis?"

"Referenced in our ancient texts."

"Good to know."

"I've come in aid of a possible alliance."

"Alliance? On what causes would you need alliances from the surface?"

"Enemies of the sea kingdoms are preparing an ambush of wars upon my kingdom and my people. I need the aid of these rising heroes to face them when the time comes."

"And you believe I am a suitable candidate for your war?"

"Yes."

"No disrespect, I have enough to deal with on the surface as do many other surface-dwellers. Best you gather those of your own kind to deal with the matters."

"You don't understand."

"I don't think you understand."

The ground trembled quickly beneath their feet. Kular looked around the darkness of the forest and a low-pitched growl was heard. The Swordman raised up his sword from its sheath, it shined as bright as the moon. The weapon was astonishing to Kular's eyes.

"What is that?"

"My choice of weaponry?"

"What's growling?"

"You're about to find out."

From the trees jumped out a troll, a large one. Nearly seven-feet in height. Its skin the color of the forest bark and its smell was of the swamp. The eyes of the troll were yellow as a kindled flame and its two horns were as tough as a ram's.

"Kular, meet the Troll."

The Troll rammed toward Kular, who held it back with his strength. The Swordman moved over, jumping over Kular and swiping the Troll on its back with the sword. The Troll turned and kicked Swordman in the chest, grabbing Kular by his head and slamming him into the ground. Dirt flew in the air as Kular kicked the Troll from him and wiped the soil from his face.

"Its strength." Kular said. "It's stronger than I would perceive."

"He's a difficult one." The Swordman replied. "That is true."

The Troll ran toward them headfirst. The horns were set to bolt them both. The Swordman flipped over the Troll as Kular held the horns in his hands. Fighting against the strength of the Troll. The Swordman moved over and impaled the Troll in the back of his neck. The Troll fell to the ground and was quickly submerged into the soil. The area became still and silent.

"That went by fast." Kular said.

"Because I know of his weakness. When it's hit, he returns to the soil. Just as fast as he appeared. The same goes for his leave."

"Is it dead?"

"No. He always finds a way to return and I will be waiting on him."

Kular took a breather.

'Look, just take my word for it. Help me in my war to protect Atlantis."

"I'll give you this. When the time comes, I will make myself known to you and to your people. Until then, I must deal with my own troubles. This land needs me and there are those who need this land."

Beeping came from The Swordman's forearm. He looked and on his foreman was a screen, the screen showed security footage of

Sir Onyx escaping Rockward Penitentiary.

"We'll meet again." Kular declared. "Be it one side or the other."

"It is already written." The Swordman said before bellowing into the shadows of the night. Only the sheathing of the sword was heard.

Kular was fully set to return to Atlantis. He left Retropolis and he would never forget the quick, yet, impressive encounter with The Swordman. The Aqua-Barbarian had believed.

IX

<u>SAVING YOUR OWN</u>

Kular entered the seas, returning to Atlantis with quick speed, moving through the waters. Upon his arrival, he discovered his kingdom is under attacked. Soldiers scattered across the gates. Floating motionless in the waters.

"What has happened?"

Kular swam faster, reaching the palace. He entered with a bolting rush of strength and found his wife Kara of Atlantis being held captive by a tentacle. Sharp, a dark green hue to the hide, its height sixteen feet, and its eyes were a gleaming, searing red. Only a malevolent essence lived within them. Its long, dark raven hair flowing with the motions of the sea. A slow brushing.

"You." Kular said.

"You remember me?" The creature mentioned. "How quaint of you."

"How are you here?"

"A wonder only fit for those who desire certain knowledge."

"Tell me."

"Why should I tell you. You know of me. Of my nature. My name."

"I know what you are, and I know your name."

"Say it."

"You're Ark. The Sea Monster."

"Yes. I am Ark, the Sea Monster. Your forefathers called me the Sea Demon. I prefer the latter much more than being called a monster. I am truly a sea demon."

"You've broken sacred laws by entering my kingdom and taking a hold of my wife."

"I don't abide by your rules. I am above your laws. The laws of the sea and the laws of the land."

"I will kill you."

"Many have tried, boy. You'll just be another one on the long list of those who dared to destroy me."

Kular extended his arms and from across the room came his trident. Glowing with lightning and searing with energy. Ark released Kara from his hold and she fell to the floor. Crawling over to the side of the room as Kular and Ark measured one another.

"You're leaving me with no other option but to kill you."

"Don't mind me, there are others on the way."

Horns blared from across the waters, near the front of the kingdom. Kular turned, hearing them. He turned back toward Ark who was laughing with a sinister grin. Kular threw his trident toward him and Ark liquefied his body as the trident went through him and slammed into the wall.

"See you around, King of the Seas!" Ark yelled as he swam away.

Kular approached Kara as he helped her on her feet. They stood there, seeing the other remaining Atlantean soldiers making moves near the front gates.

"He's coming, my love."

"Who's coming?"

"Lord Shark. He's the one who freed Ark. He's coming to take the kingdom from you."

"He won't. believe me."

Kara nodded with a smile. She was certain.

"Where's Novah?"

"He was helping others to safety. He's probably in the hall room."

Kular kissed Kara as he went to the hall.

Kular swan to the hall and he saw the crowds of Atlantean civilians. They sat amongst each other on the floors of the hall and standing around them was Novah. He gazed up, seeing Kular and ran toward him.

"Good you're back."

"I came right on time."

"Where did Ark run off to?"

"He vanished just as Lord Shark is making his way here."

"Figures. Word had to have spread concerning your battle with Sea Kaiser. Every other nations will want war with you for this place."

"And they will have it. Lord Shark will suffer the same fate as Kaiser."

Kular held his trident and went to the outside. He stood amongst his soldiers as they waited for Lord Shark and his clan of fanged ones to arrive. Another battle was set to begin.

X

<u>NOW AND COMING</u>

Lord Shark looked out among the Atlantean army and he could see Kular standing with them. His trident set in the ground. Lighting encamped around it. Lord Shark smirked with his teeth. Lord Shark himself is a hybrid of shark and Atlantean. Born from a conception banned by ancient Atlanteans. Hence his hatred for all things Atlantis.

"My fanged ones, this day we shall overcome the Atlanteans and their kingdom will be ours!"

Lord Shark swan with his army toward Atlantis. Kular raised up his trident and yelled for victory, leading the Atlantean army into battle. The two armies collided with weapons of war. The slashing and impaling was astounding. Blood flowed through the waters as sharks and other sea creatures circled the surroundings of the kingdom. Kular plowed his way through fanged ones to reach Lord Shark and the two stood facing one another.

"You didn't heed the warnings of Kaiser's defeat."

"I'm not Kaiser. He was too brash to take you on. I'm calm.

Still. Steadfast."

"Let us see if this battle proves your words true."

Shark slammed his axe against the trident of Kular. Both strong with strength, yet, Shark was more cunning than the Aqua-Barbarian. Shark kicked Kular in the abdomen and tripped him with the handle of the axe. Kular moved from the falling axe as it crushed into the ground. Kular twirled the trident and punched Shark, later grabbing him by his back fin and tossing him toward the gates of the kingdom.

"Letting me in. How nice."

Kular smacked Shark with the trident. Shark dodged the coming blow and grabbed Kular by his throat, slamming him into the ground. Holding his head into the sea floor.

"You can't breathe when there's no air or water in your reach."

Atlantean soldiers swam over to assist their king and were knocked down by Shark's impressive strength and the quickness of his axe. While the soldiers kept Shark busy, Kular arose and grabbed his trident. He moved with speed and jammed the trident into Shark's back. He roared in pain, causing a wave to flow under the sea. Shark kicked Kular from him and removed the trident. He began to swim away. Kular held the soldiers back.

"Let him run."

"Is he running away?" A soldier asked.

"Yeah. He is."

Shark called back his fanged ones and they retreated. All for a blow to his back, Shark couldn't take the opportunity to lose his life to an Atlantean. Atlantis celebrated their victory in battle. Given how short it was. Later in the day, Novah approached Kular in his study.

"The battle was short."

"All due to Shark's fear of death. Next time, it will be his last."

"Hmm." Novah chuckled.

"Is there something else you need to ask me, advisor?"

"There is. What did you find when you visited the surface world?"

"Allies. Adversaries. Hope. Fear. War."

"All of them?"

"All of them. I just hope they understand what's coming. It won't affect only the seas. But, the land and the sky."

"Give them time. The humans are just settling with the notion of the rising heroes. The world is just giving into it for the moment. Once they're settled, the heroes will call for us to aide them in the troubles that await all the world."

"We can only hope."

"We will." Novah declared.

He left the King to his study. Kular grabbed a book from the shelves and opened it. within the book was the insignia of The Swordman, the symbol of Commander Norland, cases of nubreeds, studies of life living amongst the sky. Even minor translations of beings from other dimensions. Kular began to study them. To learn of those who also share the earth with him and his kind.

DESTINY OF THE CHAMPIONS: THROUGHOUT THE EONS

I

<u>FORESIGHT</u>

Through the shattering light of travel, Doctor Amadeus Omega had burst into the present age of existence. He had arrived in the age of where he set. Running from Baron Eon in the far future. Omega's ship, called the Spellvector made its landing in an open field. Only a forest and mountains could be seen in the night. Omega exited his ship and looked at the surroundings.

"Let's see here." Omega said, glancing at his watch.

"Vanessa, did we make it?"

Vanessa is the A.I. of the Spellvector. Created in the future as an artificial intelligence suited and capable for time travel and warfare.

"We have landed in Present Day North America." Vanessa said. "In the United States of America."

"Oh, good." Omega chuckled. "And the date is as I set?"

"May 16, 2018"

"Right on time."

Omega went into the ship and pulled up holographic images

of details pertaining to the time and age. He smiled. Filled with hope. The holograms projected three images of individuals. Two men, African American and Hispanic, and one woman. African American as well.

"They're here in this time."

"Who's here?" Vanessa asked.

"The ones I've come to gather. They can aid us in stopping Baron Eon."

Omega prepped his ship and it began to start. Its engines letting out a smoothing sound. Not rugged or loud as an average engine. Omega entered the ship and it hovered. He sat in the cockpit. Belt buckled

"Where are we off to, sir?"

"Park Valley, Utah." Omega declared. "Time to assemble my unit."

The Spellvector bolted off in a flash of light. No longer to be seen.

The ship quickly appeared in Park Valley, Utah like a bolt of lightning hovering in the air.

"Vanessa, can you find him?"

"I already have. He's currently operating in his laboratory."

'Excellent." Omega said, getting up from his seat. "Take the wheel, Vanessa. I'll be teleporting to his location."

"Understood."

Omega turned the front of his watch and pressed a button. His body began to transform into a glowing transparent figure before vanishing. The Spellvector flew off as he teleported. Omega had found himself inside a laboratory. He was impressed by all the technology which sat within the walls. Tech relatable to the timeship.

"This place is miraculous."

Omega walked through the laboratory, seeing scientists and they stared at him. Yet, didn't take a cause for concern, due to Omega wearing a white scientist coat and dressed as one. Omega turned a corner and saw a young man working on an exo-suit in a room. Omega approached the door and knocked.

"Sorry to disturb you."

The young man turned quickly and faced Omega.

"Who are you?"

"I am a friend. Not yet, anyhow. But, I know you and I know your future."

"That's good to know. You're a fortune teller or something?"

"No. I'm not."

"Then, why are you here? How did you manage to get back here?"

"I'm a scientist. Not only by dress. No, no. I am a true scientist. A genuine one."

"That doesn't quite answer the question."

"Ok. Let me explain everything. My name is Amadeus Omega and you're Corbin Beval."

"How do you know my name?"

"Give me a few moments of your time and I will tell you all."

Corbin nodded and pointed toward the door. Omega closed the door and sat at the desk near Corbin's workstation. The young man ceased from working on the suit and turned toward Omega. He exhaled.

"Ok, tell me what you have to say."

"You won't believe me when I tell you-"

"Say it anyway. You're here now."

"I am not from your era."

"Pardon? What?"

"I am from the future. I operate as a science engineer. Sometimes as a time doctor."

"What's a time doctor? And what do you mean you come from the future?"

"I come from a future where this era's history is profound. The events which unfold during this age is unbelievable, yet sound in the art of time and space."

"I'm not understanding any of this and I'm a scientist."

"Trust me, where I'm from, you've learned. Learned so much than you can possibly imagine."

"And why have you chosen to come to the past? Your past and visit me?"

"That suit you're working on. It works."

"You've seen it?"

"Not only have I seen it. I've seen it used in battles of war. In tools of protection. Even in a game of tug-a-war."

"So, it works as I intended?"

"More than you intended. With the suit, you've saved countless lives and became a hero amongst the heroes."

"You're saying my dream is a reality in the future?"

"More than a reality."

"That's good news for me."

"Figured it would be so."

"But, why come to see me?"

"I need your help."

"My help with what?"

"Stopping a threat from erupting the time stream as we know it."

"You mean taking down a bad guy?"

"Something along those lines. Yeah."

"I can't help you there."

"How come? I've told you what you'll do in the future. Why is it such a problem now?"

"Because, I'm not aware of my capabilities yet. I know what the suit can do. But, can I do more with it."

"I've already told you what you're capable of with the suit."

"Why visit me when you can go anywhere in time. There are others whose skills are vast enough to work with. Why me?"

"Because you will join in the ranks of the other rising heroes and together will shape the earth anew. As I've heard from many in the past, have a little faith."

Corbin nodded. Hanging his head. Omega sighed.

"I'll be outside by the ship. You have a choice. Either come with me or stay here. Create a better future for all or remain working in your laboratory. Your choice."

Omega walked out of the lab. Leaving Corbin to meditate on the offer. Omega waited outside and from across the lab, Corbin walked out, carrying a bag. He spotted the Spellvector, yet no sound emitted from it. It startled him for a second as he paused and pointed. The size of the ship surpassed his expectations.

"It's been only thirty minutes, Mr. Beval."

"That's a timeship?"

"It is."

"How come it isn't making any sound?"

"Smoothness of future tech. engines no longer roar as they do in your present era."

"Apparently so."

"You've made your decision?"

"Yeah. I'll come along. Just to see what I'm capable of and what can be done to make a better future."

Omega nodded with a smile. "Excellent. Let's get going to gather the other two."

"Other two?" Corbin wondered.

"Yes. You weren't the only one I came back in time for."

"Do you know where they are currently?"

"In a spark of time, I do."

Omega and Corbin travel through lightspeed, ending up in Los Angeles, California. The ship hovered over a prison. Corbin looked out of the window, seeing the prison grounds and immediately sat down.

"What's wrong?" Omega asked.

"Why are we at a prison?"

"There's someone here I've come to get."

"You mean you're going to break an inmate out of prison?"

"Precisely. The guards won't notice a thing."

"How?"

"I'm from the future. We have ways of making people

disappear.”

Omega opened the door, looking down at the prison and its size. Beval was uncertain as he glanced over, looking out.

“You know where to find him in there?”

“Won’t take long.” Omega noted. “I’ll be back. Stay with the ship.”

Omega pressed his watch and teleported from the ship to the interior of the prison. Inside, he saw the prisoners sitting in their cells. They looked at him strangely and confusion was all that came to mind.

“No trouble.” Omega said. “Just looking for a friend.”

Omega reached near the end of the hall and stopped at a cell. He inched closer. Staring at the man. A man of Hispanic descent. His prison clothes were covered with red lines. He looked over, seeing Omega standing at his cell, staring.

“Something you want?”

“Yes. You.”

“I don’t swing that way, my friend.”

“That’s not what I was implying.”

“Then, who the hell are you and why are you staring at me?”

“It’s a long story.”

“Make it short, then.”

“Fine. I’m here to break you out.”

The man stood still and grinned.

“Open the gate.”

Omega pulled out a pen, pointing it at the door. The pen began emitting an energy laser, slicing the door from its hinges. The door fell outward and the man walked out of his cell.

"Who are you?"

"Someone who needs your help."

Omega looked over near the doors and sees the security approaching. Moving fast, Omega teleported himself and the man out of the prison. Beval sat on the ship and behind him appeared Omega and the prisoner.

"That didn't take long."

"Who's he?" The prisoner asked.

"He's with me."

"So, why did you break me out?"

"I will tell you." Omega said. "Once we find our last member."

"Another one?" Beval asked.

"Yes. She will prove very useful to the cause."

"She?" Beval noticed.

"Yes. We're heading to Tennessee now."

The Spellvector took off from above the prison and transferred the group to Nashville, Tennessee. The ship sat above the countryside. Hovering over a grass field. Beval and the prisoner looked out of the windows toward the ground.

"I don't see anyone down there?" Beval said.

"Same."

"One thing, what is your name?" Beval asked the prisoner.

"Antonio Carlos. Those who know me call me Crimson Mask."

"Crimson Mask? For what reason?"

"He's a mercenary." Omega said. "One of the skillful ones I will add."

"How do you know that?"

"I will explain once I find her. She's somewhere beneath us."

"We don't see anyone, man."

Beval looked and on the ground, he saw a horse and atop the horse was a woman. A woman who's bronze-skin shined against the sun. She was riding the horse through the field.

"Is that her?" Beval pointed.

"It is." Omega added, looking out. "I'll be right back. Don't go anywhere."

"We don't know how to operate this thing." Anthony said.

"One day you will."

As the woman rode the horse, she noticed a large shadow looming over the field gazing up, she found herself staring at the Spellvector.

"The hell?"

Just as the horse stopped, Omega appeared in front of her. Startling her and the horse.

"Don't fear me, miss. I've come with some urgent news."

"Who are you and how did you just appear out of thin air?"

"I can explain. But, first I need you to come with me."

"I don't deal with strangers."

"I'm not a stranger."

"I don't know who you are."

"Someday you will, and it starts today."

"How could I ever trust you?"

"I know what you can do. The strength you possess. It's

unheard-of in these lands. Minus the others who roam about."

"How do you know about–"

"Your strength. I know a lot about you Sandra Banks. Please, come with me and I'll explain everything."

Sandra nodded and returned the horse to her home and joined Omega on the ship. Beval and Anthony stared at her as she entered. The three sat together as Omega stood in front of them.

"This might come as a shock, but I'm from the future."

"Huh?" Anthony asked.

"The future?" Sandra referenced.

"It's true." Beval said.

"The reason I've brought the three of you together is for the sole purpose of protecting your futures. There is a man out there named Baron Eon and he is seeking to change all of time and history. But, with your help, I can find a way to stop him and end his desire for change period."

"So, he's a threat to our lives?" Anthony asked.

"A grave threat."

"How would we go about stopping someone like him?" Beval asked.

"Because as I am aware, I know of each of your feats. Beval's exo-suit and the energy it obtains. Anthony skillful tactics and senses of stealth, and Sandra's excessive strength and agility. The three of you possess gifts much of the world sorely desires, but don't desire enough. With me, as a time-traveler and scientist, we can accomplish this mission and save the future for countless lives."

Beval nodded. Anthony smirked, and Sandra shook her head.

Omega took each of their notions as a sign of agreement.

"So, where are we headed next?" Beval asked.

"To the Northern West of Canada. In 1875."

Omega sat down in the cockpit and pulled the lever, transferring them to the year 1875. Across the stars of space, Baron Eon rode in his own version of the Spellvector. A black-and-blue ship covered with sleekness that even the stars marvel at its appearance. In the ship are several armed men.

"How far are we?" Eon asked.

"We are on their trail, sir." An armed man said.

"Excellent." Eon grinned. "It won't be long before Amadeus' head is beneath my foot.

II

<u>THE NORTHERN WEST</u>

The Spellvector moved with haste and a quickening speed, launching the team into the year 1875. The ship calmed as it exited the time-warp and entered the atmosphere of the Northern West region of Canada.

"We've arrived." Omega said. "1875."

The team looked out through the windows, seeing the wide, open field lying beneath them. Several homes could be seen, yet, no one was walking about on the ground. Ahead of them was a small city.

"Where are we headed?" Beval asked.

"Silver City. It's where we must go."

"Why?" Sandra asked.

"It's the perfect place to find out what I need."

"Exactly, why are we here to begin with?" Anthony wondered. "Why are we truly in the west of the past?"

"Let me explain."

Omega placed the ship on autopilot and approached the wall. A wall made of a clear, yet durable material. Omega tapped the wall and it lit up. Forming holographic words and images. The team sat in front of it as Omega had hoped. On the wall, formed an image of Baron Eon.

"Who's that?"

"He's called Baron Eon. He's from my time."

"Is that why we're here?" Sandra asked.

"Yes. He is after me and I needed to come here in order to slow him down."

"How do you know he's slowing down from your trail?"

"I just know. Or I hope."

"So, why did you recruit us?" Beval asked.

"Because you're the team who will help me defeat him and protect your coming futures."

"How?"

"You become more than what you appear to be. You become heroes. Champions."

"Heroes?" Anthony mocked.

"Champions?" Beval asked. "Like those military brats with Commander Norland?"

"Heroes? Yes. Champions like Norland's team? No. You're champions of something more. Something vast."

"What?"

"The future."

"And you needed us for this whole thing? How come you didn't ask The Resistance to assist you?"

"Their future is already in motion. Yours however is just beginning to unfold."

Omega shut down the holographic wall and stood in front of

the team, grabbing his white laboratory coat.

"The ship will land in this open field while we walk toward Silver City. It's only a few miles away."

"And again, why are we going into the city?"

"For reasons that concern Eon. Also, I hear there's someone in this time-period who could provide some assistance in our cause."

Anthony nodded and stood up from his seat.

"Then let's get going."

"We're going to need to dress the part if we're going to survive the city."

"Sure." Beval said. "You don't have any Old West clothing lying around do you?"

"I have enough."

Omega approached a closet and he opened the doors, revealing a crowded room of clothes from various time periods. From the past, the present, and the future. Omega walked toward a door, opening it. The team looked on as Omega moved out of the way.

"Pick something."

The team picked the clothing which interests them and as Omega waited outside, the team appeared, dressed in Old West clothing. Omega nodded with a smile.

"Splendid."

"How did you retrieve all those clothes?" Beval asked.

"Much traveling. Plus, research."

The team went on and entered Silver City. A place crowded

with men atop horses and women moving throughout the streets. The stench in the air was unbearable to the team, except for Omega.

"The smell is terrible." Sandra said.

"It's of the times, my dear."

As they walked, a man stepped in front of them. He was dressed in all brown clothing with a black duster and hat. His face was calm, yet, cold at the same time. His eyes were locked onto the team before cutting over to Omega. Omega looked at the man and, in an instant, he smirked.

"I know you." Omega uttered.

"As I you." The man replied. "You must be the one."

"I am. Doctor Amadeus Omega."

"The time-traveler."

"That would be me."

"And is this your crew?"

"My partners. They are my parents in this dire cause."

"So, I see."

"Can we talk somewhere more privately?"

"Follow me. And keep your eyes to yourselves. Don't look at anybody suspicious unless you want a fight on your hands."

They followed the man in black over to the saloon, where they entered and approached the back of the place. They sat down and had a section to themselves away from the few people who were drinking inside.

"Now, I need to know." Omega said. "Are you the guy they talked about?"

"Talked about how?"

"You know. The guy who took down those men in hats some time ago all by himself."

"That would be me."

"You're Clint Winston?" Beval uttered. "The Lone Outlaw?"

"You're looking at him, lad."

"Wait, he's the guy who went around killing those criminals?" Sandra asked.

"That's me." Clint said with a grin. "I do what others refuse. They fear those guys in power. I don't."

"The words of an outlaw." Omega said.

"Getting back to your time-traveling business, I was sent word about your adversary, Baron Eon tracking you throughout the timeline."

"Yes. I was informed you can help by slowing Eon down."

"That I can do."

"How can you do that?" Anthony said. "If I may ask."

"My skill set is equipped to take out anyone I come across. No matter the time periods or age."

"Good to know." Beval said.

"Now, can you tell me how you can help in taking down Eon?"

"Simple. Use your skill set in ways you've never thought before."

"What?" Eon asked. "What do you mean by that?"

"Eon already knows your moves. Your motives. Your tricks. You're going to have to maneuver a technique unknown to even him. Otherwise, you and your team will end up in the ground and Eon will have gained control over time itself."

"I'm not sure of any other motives I might have."

"Best begin to look for them."

Someone walked toward their table from around the corner of the saloon. He stood close to the table, dressed in all brown clothing. From his hat to the duster and boots. He smirked at Omega and his team and nodded toward Winston.

"Why are you here, Thaine?"

"I didn't know you had friends around these lands. Especially with the way they're looking."

"How do we look?" Beval wondered.

"Like outsiders. Outsiders from somewhere else. Not familiar with us or our status quo."

"You're Thaine Tucker." Beval said. "The Thaine Tucker?"

"At your service, sir."

"Why are you standing here?" Winston asked.

"Because, I don't find it kind to see you talking with outsiders in this saloon and in this part of the place. It's too quiet. Spooky."

"You're the one who's unsettling."

"Same can be said of you, Lone One."

"Sorry, we want no trouble." Omega said. "Clint is just assisting us with some business."

"Ah, business. What kind of business may I ask?"

"Dealing with time."

"Time? Oh, how so? Time in the brothel? Drinking games? Taking out the authorities?"

"It concerns none of those things." Winston said. "Again, why are you here, Thaine?"

"In short, to warn these people. These strange people to get away from you before harm comes to them."

"They'll be well." Winston said.

"They will?"

"We can handle ourselves." Anthony said. "No disrespect."

"I see."

"Best you leave now." Winston said to the team. "Get yourself from this troublemaker."

"Troublemaker?" Thaine uttered. "I'm not the one who's causing the trouble."

Omega stood up from the table as did the team. He nodded.

"We should be leaving anyway." Omega said. "There's no telling what Eon may be up to at the moment."

"I agree." Winston said. "I will walk you all out."

Clint walked the team out of the saloon and Thaine followed. Keeping his eyes on Winston and the team. Once they're outside, a wisp of cold air consumed the area. An unsettling chill touched the skin of all who stood outside. Their breath became visible.

"Something's not right." Winston said.

"You can tell?" Omega asked.

"I always know when something isn't what it seems."

In the distant stood a figure of a man, cloaked in all black and dark blue clothing. His footsteps created ice beneath his feet and his face was covered by a mask and hood. Yet, his eyes were glaring as blue as the sky. Sandra turned, seeing the figure and pointed.

"Who is that?"

The team looked, seeing the figure walking toward them. Clint stood next to Omega as they stared at the figure.

"Who's he supposed to be?" Clint asked. "A friend?"

"Not one of ours." Omega said. "Perhaps, he's with Eon."

The figure faced them and raised his hands. From them appeared glowing shards of ice. Twirling in the air. He held them up, facing the team.

"You and your team need to go." Clint said. "I'll deal with this iceman."

"Are you sure?" Omega asked. "We can assist."

"No need. I'll keep him busy for you to return to your ship."

Omega nodded. "Understood. We'll meet again."

"As planned in the times to come."

Omega and the team made a move to return to their ship. By doing so, the tall figure began to run after them. Clint jumped in between the two opposing forces and started firing at the figure. The team continued running with Omega looking back at Clint shooting at the figure. The figure threw the ice shards toward Clint, who crushed them with his six-shooters in the air.

"Ah, what the hell." Thaine said, shooting at the figure.

Clint and Thaine stood together to face the figure and Omega ran back to his team. They arrived at the ship and entered. Omega ran for the cockpit and once he sat down, the ship levitated and hovered in the air. On the ground, Clint and Thaine were fighting the figure with their six-shooters and their feet.

"Have they left yet?" Thaine asked.

Clint turned back and, in the sky, he saw the ship bolt with quick speed into the atmosphere. He turned back to Thaine.

"They're gone."

As the Spellvector traveled throughout time, Omega checked on the identity of the ice figure. Upon his research, he discovered the figure is referred to in the present era as the Dark Snowman.

"Eon sent him." Omega said. "He knows where we are and where we're going."

III

<u>COSMICBOX</u>

The Spellvector jolted from its travel and placed the team back into present day. Omega continued working in his office and Beval entered, seeing Omega busy with many documents laying around his workspace.

"Did you find something?"

"I did." Omega said. "That iceman we saw back in 1875 is known as the Dark Snowman and he's from the present era."

"Then, why was he back in the Northern West period?"

"I believe Eon contacted him to be a muscle. Placed him in 1875 because he knew that's where we were heading."

"He's tracking us?"

"It's a high probability that I would like to assume and not confirm at the moment."

"Should I tell the others?"

"No. I will tell them."

Omega gathered the team together and told them of the Dark Snowman's appearance along with the possibility of Eon keeping track of them by unknown means. The team were displeased with the news as could be so.

"Anyway, why are we back in modern day?" Anthony asked.

"There's an object we need that can help us defeat Eon. Thanks to Clint's connections, we've managed to find the location of this object."

"What is the object?" Sandra asked.

The screen clicked on and the team could see the holographic image of a box. A cube-shaped box, glowing with red glints of light in between the lining.

"It's called a cosmicbox." Omega said. "A very rare object from what I've studied."

"And what are we going to do with it?" Beval wondered. "Is there a way to stop Eon with it?"

"There is." Omega confirmed. "And all we have to do is get the box in our possession before Eon gets to it."

Omega walked toward the cockpit and the team sat. The Spellvector took off to another location in the present era. The warehouse. The team ejected from the ship, dressed as spies as they approached the warehouse. The surroundings were silent and there was hardly anyone around. Omega nodded at the scenery and the quietness.

"The box is contained within the building."

"How do we get in?" Anthony asked.

"Simple."

Omega pressed a button on his watch and instantly teleported himself and the team into the warehouse. The team jolted, shaking themselves from the teleporting effect to their bodies.

"You could've warned us." Anthony said.

"I could've. But, it's best to just do it."

Beval glanced around the interior of the warehouse, discovering it's full of robotic technology. Amazed as he was when he attempted to touch some of the tech before Omega grabbed his arm.

"Don't touch anything. We can't leave any changes behind."

"You see all of this tech?"

"I do. We're not here for that. We're here for the cosmicbox. Wherever it is."

Crashing noises started to bang across the warehouse near the team and from a nearby window appeared a woman. Dressed in all black clothing, a tank top shirt, fingerless gloves, cargo pants and leather boots with her long blonde hair in a ponytail down her back. She turned around, seeing the team. Omega noticed in her arms was the cosmicbox itself.

"No way." Omega said.

"Isn't that the box?" Anthony asked.

"It is."

The woman glanced at the team and the box. She scoffed.

"Are you here for this?"

"We are." Omega said. "Miss?"

"Tessa Balthazar. Famed treasure huntress."

"Well, Ms. Balthazar, we're on an important message and we require that box you're trying to escape with."

"Will you pay me if I hand it to you?"

"No, we won't."

"Well, as much as I would like to help, this box will sell for trillions at the market share."

"I think not." Anthony said.

Anthony raised up two handguns and started firing them toward Tessa. She dodged the bullets and ran across the floor through the robotic tech. Anthony continued firing as Tessa inched closer.

"She's coming closer." Beval noticed.

Tessa jumped in front of Anthony, kicking the guns from his hands before smashing the box across his head. She kicked Sandra as Beval attempted to snatch the box from her. She pulled it back and stared.

"How rude of you!"

"You're the one stealing it!" Beval replied.

Tessa punched Beval and shoved him to the floor. Omega jumped in front of her, grabbing a hold of the box. The two pulled back and forth for the box as it began to hum loudly and glow with a red hue.

"What is it doing?" Beval asked.

"We're about to find out." Tessa said.

The box shook in their arms and emitted a blast of energy, which knocked Tessa and the team on the ground. The dust had started to descend on the ground. Omega looked up and saw the box sitting motionless on the floor and Tessa inching her way to retrieve it. As her fingers come close to touching the box, a large portal opened with an early boom. Omega glanced as the portal opened wider.

"He's here." Omega said.

"Who?" Sandra asked.

From the portal walked out Baron Eon. He stood tall above

the team and Tessa and glanced down, seeing the cosmicbox in front of him. He bent down and grabbed it. Holding it with power in his hands.

"No." Omega said.

"How fitting is this, Amadeus. To see what you've come to collect only end up in my hands. As with everything before."

"Give us the box!" Beval said, holding up a device from his pocket. Attached to his wrist, the device fired an energy blast, which Eon caught in his hand.

"How primitive your weapons are. I've managed to forget your era's weakness in weaponry."

"You can't do this, Eon."

"Oh, I can and I'm going to."

Eon returned to the portal with Omega standing up to chase him. Omega came close as the portal shut. Silence filled the warehouse and the team looked at one another. Omega looked around, not seeing Tessa, yet, to only find an open window. He shook his head.

"We almost had it."

"There's still a way to track it down." Sandra said. "We track down the box, we find Eon."

"You're right."

"If it wasn't for that blonde bitch, we would've got out of here with the box." Anthony said.

"Maybe so."

"There's no maybe in this. We had the damn thing. Came right on time and what happened. She was in our way and ruined our mission. She's lucky she escaped before we came to our grips."

"Sandra is right." Omega said. "We'll return to the ship and track down the box. Finish this before any more harm is done."

The group had searched for Baron Eon continually. Eventually, they learned he had vanished through space and time. Not knowing his current whereabouts.

YONDERERS: ALIENATION

I

DO NOT CONFORM TO THIS WORLD

Professor Cullen Edge sat with the Yonderers in the mansion where they reside near the city of Chicago. Within the library, he sat at a desk, in front of him were Marth Randolph, Jr., known as Valinor, Scott Branagh, known as Emerald, Danny Blake, known as Hailstone, Lois Frost, Ariana Cerra, known as Gale, Isabel Dotson, known as Magic Carpet, and Daniel Summers, known as The Surf.

"Listen to me very closely." Edge said to the group. "Do not conform to this world."

"How come?" Daniel asked.

"Because you're not like them."

"Not human, you mean?" Danny said.

"You're human. But, a higher version of humanity. All of you possess abilities which majority of humanity do not possess."

"That's why we're hated amongst them." Isabel said. "Isn't it?"

Edge hung his head low before facing her. Lois turned toward her with a nod.

"Yes, it is."

"Which is why you will all reside here, in this mansion of mine."

"When do we continue to go out and help people?" Scott asked.

"Wow. I didn't know you really wanted to help them." Marth uttered. "I thought we would probably take a moment before facing the threats that are posed before us."

"Threats?" Scott asked.

"General Rilla." Edge said. "and his group of nubreeds."

"He has his own lair?" Danny asked. "Like this one?"

"Not exactly. But, he does have a team and what I am teaching all of you concerning the world we live in, he is teaching them the opposite. Whereas I teach you to save and protect, Raymus teaches his to kill and destroy."

"So, what's our plan when we have to confront him, boss?" Marth asked.

"We try to solve things without violence."

"But, from what I've learned, General Rilla is all for violence.

"Indeed, Marth. He is."

Edge continued to teach the Yonderers concerning their lives amongst humanity and the other potential threats which roam across the world. From unseen nubreeds to the rising heroes and their adversaries.

"Just remember what I've told you this day. Do not conform to this world."

II

DECIMATE THE PATTERN OF THIS WORLD

In another place far from the Yonderers Mansion, General Rilla gathered his own nubreed recruits, forming the Fellowship of Nubreeds. Rilla stood before them in an old and worn-out facility in the outskirts of Chicago. A facility once used to manufacture weapons for both World Wars. Rilla is dressed in his warrior uniform, only thing missing is his helmet, modeled after the Soviet hats worn by generals during World War II.

Sitting before Rilla are Cosmic Card, Mistress Destroyer, Omega Thunder, X-Manta, The Marine, Eerie, and Jackhammer. Together, they form General Rilla's Fellowship of Nubreeds. Each wield different traits. Making them perfect for a team whose goal is to gain the attention of the world populace.

"Listen closely, my brothers and sisters. We must bring forth a plan to make humanity learn our demands. We are superior to them. Our kind possess feats capable of wiping out all the humans. If need be, that will be our only option."

"There aren't any other choices for them to decide?" Cosmic

Card asked.

"What other choices do they have?"

"Not many according to what you're telling us. Are they as evil as you propose?"

Rilla moved himself from his position and approached Card. Standing over him with purpose and fear began to sink into Card, to which he went further down in his seat as Rilla hovered over him. Staring with his glowing dark violet eyes.

"As I shall continue."

Rilla returned to his previous position and continued telling his Fellowship of his plans for the world and for humanity. Some disagreed internally with Rilla's decisions, yet they understood his reasons and agreed to assist him in making his dream a reality.

Later during the evening, Rilla was visited by Edge in his lair. Edge looked around at the place, seeing its aged nature. He nodded with a faint smile. Rilla was unimpressed by Edge's sudden appearance.

"Why have you come?" Rilla asked.

"I've come to speak to you for a short moment. I have a proposal."

"What kind of proposal?"

"One for all nubreeds alike."

Rilla grabbed a chair from the wall and sat down facing Edge. Edge himself was already sitting in a chair near the door of the room.

"I'm listening."

"It would be best for the two of us to speak somewhere else. Somewhere your recruits shall not hear of our discussion."

"And what of yours? Your "Yonderers". That's what you're calling yourselves? Sharing team names like those others.

"We are not like the others. You know it better than most."

"Then, why aren't you and your team siding with me? Together, we can make this world ours. A world fit for nubreeds. Humans have had their time in the sun and now it is our time to mark it with the darkness of the night."

"Meet me at an undisclosed location tomorrow. There we can dig further into our opposites views."

"Why? Why do this now? I've told you for years what side I'm on. I think it's time you look and see for yourself what a big mistake you're making."

Edge stood up and walked toward the door. He stopped and turned to Rilla.

"Meet me tomorrow and prove me wrong." Edge smirked.

"Very well, old friend." Rilla said. "That I will do."

Edge left the room with Rilla sitting. Meditating as dark electricity began to surround him. His eyes started to glow as his meditation increased.

III

<u>DECISIONS</u>

Edge and Rilla have both arrived at the undisclosed location. Both alone, without their recruits. The location is an old office building. Renovation is set to begin on the building in due time as there are signs covering the grounds of the location. The two leaders stand in the center of a room, most likely the lobby area. Edge sat in the chair and Rilla only hovered. Levitating in place.

"Why are we here?" Rilla asked.

"To discuss terms."

"Terms? What terms do you have in mind?"

"For our kind to make an allegiance with humanity. To live as one. In peace."

"This argument again."

"Just here me out, Raymus."

"I will not. We've talked about this subject for years and look where it has placed the both of us. On opposite sides of the spectrum. However, I am aware the side I've chosen to be the rightful one."

"Not in my eyes you have not."

"Because you're blinded, old friend. Blinded by the ways of this world. The activities of the humans. You strive to become them. To live like them. To act like them. Soon, you and your students will fall prey to their circumstances and will look to someone like me to raise you up."

"Or we will succeed in our mission and humanity will welcome us as one of their own."

"Rilla shook his head in shame. Lowering himself to the ground. Walking around the empty lobby. He shrugged his shoulders.

"You're stubborn, Cullen. Very stubborn."

"I am optimistic of my choices."

"That is why you'll fail. Your students will fall with you."

"We will not fail, Raymus. We will succeed. Humanity will welcome us and when that is done. Humans and nubreeds will live amongst the earth as one people. No discrimination. No hatred. Only just. Only love."

"Despicable. You fail to see the truth in all of this."

"How would I?"

"Because, everything you've just said is a lie. Lying to yourself, your students, and to all nubreeds scattered across the world. If we brought ourselves out there amongst the humans, they would chain us up and treat us like animals. Put us in cages."

"No, they won't."

"How do you know?!"

"Trust me this once. That's all I'm asking."

Rilla hung and shook his head in disappointment for his old

friend. He turned and gave him a clear and depressing look. A show of failure.

"I cannot place interest in a fool's errand. You want all of us to become humanity's slaves. I am trying to set my people free. Harmony and dominion is what I crave for all nubreeds."

"We yourself as their sole ruler."

"There must be a balance to everything in existence, Cullen. Something you've failed nosecone before in the past. I am fit to rule. I have the power to do so. The mind. The will. The fortitude."

"You're calling for a dictatorship."

"It's ruler-ship. A world made peace for all nubreeds."

"A world where peace will not exist for all kinds."

"I'm not interested in all kinds. I am only concerned about my people. Nubreeds. You've seen what is happening across the world. Rising heroes appearing everywhere. Making this world safer for humanity, but troubling for nubreeds. My goal is simple. I will unite every nubreed I come across and in time, I will take the battle to the heroes and the war to humanity. In the end, I will be standing victorious with those who have chosen to follow me as I follow my mission."

"You're going mad, Raymus."

"Mad is another term for a genius mind. Every genius is considered mad. Remember when the humans called you mad for your great intellect. Knowing when things would happen before they were set in stone? Or have you forgotten the hatred they've given you?"

"If we do not come to terms in this room, there will be a war amongst nubreeds. Something I clearly do not desire."

"You're choosing to side with humanity. By that statement, you have already chosen war."

Edge stood up from his seat and confronted Rilla. The two friends standing toe to toe. Rilla is more built physically than his old friend. Edge relies on his intellect to do the work for him."

"Terms, Raymus." Edge said. "This is my final time asking."

"Then, you've wasted time making this meeting."

Rilla levitated above the ground, looking down at Edge. Rilla's power began to manifest as dark violet lighting appeared from his hands and circulated his body. His eyes started to glow. Edge stood still, only staring in shame of his friend.

"We will meet again, old friend. And when we do, there will be a battle. Your Yonderers against my Fellowship. Only one side will come out the victor and it will be mine."

"You're making a mistake, Raymus."

"I am making a promise."

Rilla bolted out of the facility through a sudden teleportation effect. Leaving Edge alone in the silent building. Edge sighed as he turned toward the door and exited.

IV

<u>OF OUR OWN KIND</u>

The following day, Professor Edge and the Yonderers went out and stepped upon an open field. Surrounded only by the forests. On the other end of the field appeared General Rilla and his Fellowship of Nubreeds. They were anxious and full of vigor. The Yonderers were the same, except calmer and more collective. Both groups made steady move, inching closer toward the other. Edge and Rilla stood in the front.

"You came." Rilla said.

"We didn't come to fight." Edge said. "We're here to discuss terms."

"We've already had this conversation, old friend. Why bother doing this again?"

"For the sake of every nubreed in this world."

"If I had things my way, all nubreeds would join me in my desire to shape this world and make it a peaceful living for all of us."

"By exterminating all of humanity."

"Precisely. It's the only way to gain peace in a world such as this."

"Your speech resembles those who have gone on before us. Ancient kings spoke the same concerning their empires. And where are those empires now, Raymus?"

"I am not like those kings. I am a man with a vision. A purpose. A drive. A desire. A hope."

"Your hope will only end with many deaths and most importantly, a failure to your name."

Rilla chuckled and without a slight move, he bolted Edge with a strike of lightning from his hand. Edge fell to the ground, holding his chest and staring at Rilla.

"The choice is made!" Rilla yelled. "Fellowship! Eliminate these traitors."

The Fellowship ran towards the Yonderers. Their power showing after every quick step. Lois ran over to Edge as he stood up from the blast.

"What should we do?" Lois asked.

"Give them a battle they will never forget."

Lois nodded and turned to the team. Valinor moved forward, twirling his staff. He looked back at the team with a smile on his face.

"What are you waiting for? Let's kick their asses!"

The Yonderers and Fellowship clashed with their might. The battle escalated across the field. Lois combated with Mistress Destroyer, ice against steel. Emerald and Hailstone teamed up to battle Cosmic Card and Omega Thunder. Thunder used his electric whips to strike Emerald, yet, his mineral-hide shielded him from the lightning strikes. Valinor faced X-Manta as he began shooting at him. Valinor blocked the incoming bullets by twirling his staff. The gunshots ceased and Valinor stared. Smirking.

"Try again." Valinor scoffed.

The Surf faced The Marine. Yet, Surf found the whole scenario comedic. The Marine's brute strength was strong enough to knock a tree down and the Surf dodged the incoming strikes by emitting water from his hand, creating a hydro blast, knocking the Marine back. Gale circled around Jackhammer, a large and brute man. His footsteps quaked the ground. Gale conjured up a forceful wind to blow him to the ground, yet, he did not fall. his balance was steady.

"I am not some normal man, woman!"

"I am aware."

The final two were Magic Carpet and Eerie. Isabel flew on her carpet to avoid Eerie's magic blasts. She landed and stared at Eerie. Eerie only laughed, taking small steps toward Isabel.

"Why are you with us?" Eerie asked. "You could be so much more. We can be so much more."

"I'm well enough where I'm at." Isabel said as the carpet flew over and rolled itself around Eerie's body. Causing her to fall and strangle against it.

"Didn't see that coming." Isabel said.

In the distance of the field, Edge and Rilla stood side by side. Overseeing the battle between their units. Rilla watched closely. Studying the Yonderers. Edge monitored the battle Just as close.

"Is this what you want, Raymus?" Edge asked. "A future where our kind battle once another?"

"No." Rilla said. "I desire a future where we join forces. Take out the threat known as humanity and create a safe and peaceful world for all nubreeds. A new Eden.”

“You won’t achieve such a goal by letting this go by. By increasing such rage.”

“Your students are formidable.” Rilla said. “How will I bring them over to my cause, old friend? Without killing you that is?”

“You won’t. Because they’ve already chosen their side.”

Edge clapped his hand and a sonic wave spread through the field. The battle ceased as everyone went to cover their ears. All were affected except for Rilla, due to his helmet. He looked over to Edge and shook his head in shame.

“Still the same man from past times.”

“A better man than the one I once knew.”

“Then, I give you this warning. The battle may be over. But the war must go on.”

“Very well. Take your Fellowship and leave this place. The Yonderers have won by forfeit.”

“I’ll give you this one. For once.”

Rilla looked out at the field once the sonic wave ceased. He held his left hand in the air.

“Fellowship, cease yourselves and return home. Give this battle to the betrayers. For we shall have the war!”

The Fellowship moved swiftly, returning toward Rilla. The Yonderers stood by with confusion and uncertainty.

“I thought we were supposed to continue fighting?” Surf said.

“Doesn’t look that way.” Lois replied.

“What has he done?” Valinor wondered.

The Fellowship moved on. Rilla stopped and turned to Edge.

"The shame you will feel in the future will be far deadlier than a regular death."

Rilla left with his Fellowship as the Yonderers came to Edge's side.

"What's going on?" Lois asked.

"We're going home."

"Wait. that's it?" Surf asked. "What about those guys?"

"Another day."

The Yonderers left the fiend, but little did they know, it was near an old facility. The same facility used by Agency X.

Meanwhile at another location, military officials sat in an office and standing in front of them is a general.

"Good afternoon, you know my name as General Chazenian Cenathos and today, I have a proposition to make. We've seen the sudden appearances of this rising heroes and now with the proposed 'nubreeds' running amok, I've figured we should do something about it. I've teamed up with Ezekiel McKnight and Glasco, Inc. to begin a project that will protect us from any threat.

"And this project is?"

On the screen behind Cenathos appeared a diagram of an army. Machines. Humanoid, but larger.

"*Project Steeler*, gentlemen."

ENFORCEMENT ORDER 66: ASSEMBLING THE ENFORCEMENT

I

PROBLEM, REACTION, SOLUTION

A police car swoops pass bystanders through the rainy city of Retropolis with a lady in tow. The driver responds to his other officers that he's bringing in the lady to Pegasus Prison, where she is expected to be kept and to stay for her entire life. Approaching the tall and disturbing gate that is the entrance to Pegasus Prison, the lady in the back begins to giggle. Bothering the driving officer.

"What's so funny, lady?"

"Everything is going right as I planned. That is what's funny, sir."

"Yeah right. I'm supposed to believe a word you're saying and I'm the one taking your ass to prison. Good plan."

"This is going to be amazing!"

"What is she talking about?!"

The lady began to laugh hysterically in the car, kicking the front seats of the officers and screaming laughter.

"Quit kicking the seat!"

"I'm just having fun!"

"Where you're going, you can have all the fun you want."

"Wonderful!"

The officers arrived at Pegasus Prison where they placed Death in a more tightened cell. Death sat in the corner of the room and only giggled.

In a secret facility, Adriana Brown, known as A.B. contacted U.S. Lieutenant Gage Hark concerning the gathering for the Enforcement. Gage entered A.B.'s office with a file in his hand. Placing the file on her desk, she opened it, discovering files for perfect contenders.

"I've gathered as much Intel as I could."

"You've heard about the events that occurred in Retropolis?" A.B. asked.

"I have. Beings coming down from the sky. Something unheard of in our time."

"That is why this team will, must work. They created the problem, the world gives a reaction, and we will supply the solution."

"You're using a different kind of 'problem, reaction, solution' technique, madam."

"Better to have our own. That way, nothing will look suspicious to those with keen eyes."

"If they can all get along. Most of these guys are from different corners of the world. Different beliefs, lifestyles, you name it."

"Have you spoken with any of them?" A.B. asked.

"No ma'am." Hark said. "I expected for you to send me out to find them. Most of them aren't even in cells at the moment."

"Interesting."

A.B. closed the file and handed it back to Hark. He grabbed it as A.B. nodded.

"Recruit the ones who want to keep their lives."

"And if they refuse?"

"I'll deal with them in my own special way."

Hark nodded.

"Understood."

II

<u>WITCHES, CELEBRITIES, AND MORES</u>

Hark went out and traveled across the world, preparing to meet the potential recruits listed in the file. Hark's first location of visit was in a strange forest. The forest was lush with plant life, however, the forest relied on a powerful magic. A magic designed for nature itself. Hark walked through the forest and came upon a small cabin. Hark approached the cabin and knocked.

"Anyone here?" Hark said.

The doors opened and standing at the door was a woman wearing a long dress, all black with green lining throughout. Her long black hair was in a ponytail. She stared at Hark. Hard.

"Who are you to trespass upon my forest?"

"I am United States Lieutenant Gage Hark and I am here on military business."

"What business does a soldier possess on my land?"

"I've come to see you, Lady Silvia."

"For what purpose?"

"I am aware you know about the rising heroes across the

world."

"I know of them. What concern are they to me?"

"You don't want to find out."

"Is that why you're here?" Silvia said, approaching Hark slowly. "You've been sent to protect me?"

"I've been sent to give you an offer."

"What kind of offer?"

"One where you can use your abilities to assist those who cannot."

"Like those heroes?"

"No. Like someone who doesn't abide the law, yet, does what they wish."

"I will have to think on this offer of yours."

"Don't take too long. Anyhow, I need an answer now before I continue on."

"You'll have my answer. In time. Now, leave my domain."

Silvia raised up her arms and from the ground arose a thick, dark green mist. Hark covered his face to avoid the strong wretched stench. Running from the forest and coming out on the other side, he looked back, realizing Silvia had vanished not only herself, but her cabin.

"Clever witch." Hark said, fanning the air.

He continued moving onto the next recruits, taking his travels to Los Angeles, California. When he arrived, a movie premiere was taking place. He opened the file and read up on the potential recruit. He scoffed and closed the file.

"Got to be shitting me."

Moving through the crowd, he spotted the recruits. A young

man with slicked-back blonde hair. Wearing a white and grey fur coat with black leather pants and no shirt. His sunglasses are dark to cover his eyes from being seen by everyone else. As he approached the entrance, Hark stepped in front of him.

"Whoa. We have a problem, my boy?"

"No problem and I'm not your boy." Hark replied.

"Then, why do you stand in between me and the theater?"

"Because I know of your history and I'm here to give you an offer."

"An offer?"

"One you can't refuse."

The recruit nodded and gazed the surroundings, seeing the crowds cheering. He pointed toward the interior of the theater.

"Inside."

They entered the theater and sat in a corner where the crowds didn't notice them.

"What is this offer exactly?"

"First off, I know your name is Lance Gasper. Secondly, I know how much of a con artist you truly are."

"This some catholic session now?"

"No. your history is the reason I'm here."

"I'm not a con artist no longer."

"Then, where did you get that coat. don't remember seeing you at the Met Gala a few weeks back."

"I was refused an invitation. That's the truth."

"So you say."

"Please, tell me what you're here for and why."

"The rising heroes. Some have united together, forming a

team of their own. I have been sent by those in high places to recruit members for a team of our own. Shall I say, a team that doesn't abide the laws of civilians."

"Some kind of secret government team?"

"Yes. A shadow government team. Think Black Ops, but deeper in the shadows."

"I see. And what do these higher ups want with me?"

"Your skill set."

"Is that so?"

"True. They put you on the list for potential recruits. That is the whole reason I'm here tonight."

Lance nodded. He chuckled.

"What's in it for me?"

"Well, your past charges will be erased, and you will be completely free."

"Free?"

"Yes. No record."

Lance nodded again. He sighed and gazed around the area, seeing no one walking as they have all entered the theater room.

"Where do I sign?"

"Nowhere."

"Then, how do I join?"

Hark pulled a card from the file folder and slid it across Lance on the table. He grabbed it and read it.

"Show up at this particular address. That way, we will know you have agreed to join the team."

"When should I show up?"

"Whenever you choose."

Hark exited the theater, leaving Lance to sit and meditate on his choice.

Gage's next journey took him to a secluded island. Set afar off from the United Kingdom. The island was lush and as Hark made it ashore, he saw a woman standing at the other side of the shore, looking out at the sea.

"Just the one I'm looking for."

The woman turned and approached Hark.

"Who are you?"

"Lieutenant Gage Hark. I have come to give you a proposition."

"Proposition?"

"There's people in the higher authority, they know who you are and what you're capable of."

"And what do they require of me?"

"A chance to make this world safer."

The woman was dressed in all black. The appearance of her uniform was like leather. Although, Hark couldn't tell. Black leather with gold lining throughout her suit. Her -skin glistened across the sunlight, her dark wavy hair flowed with the coming winds. Hark pulled out a page from the file and showed it to her.

"They call you the Black Mare, right?" Hark asked.

"Yes."

III

STORMS AND LOVERS

Alcatraz, a notable maximum-security prison was renewed and remodeled after the events of the *Battle of Retropolis* with the rising heroes. Gage arrived on the island and was escorted by the security guards, dressed in black-and-white armor. Their face shielded by an silver faceplate. Hark walked down the halls of the prison, much larger and growing with prisoners every day. Gage was led down another corridor, away from the average prisoners to a small cell. The cell was glowing a shining blue from within. Gage looked inside and smirked.

"Knock-knock." Gage said.

"Move along." A voice said, coming from within the cell.

"I will as soon I have my discussion with you."

"And who are you?"

"Someone who's giving you an offer to freedom."

A figure arose from the shadows, which could be seen every second the blue light flashed. The prisoner stood at the door and Gage could see him fully. Shirtless. Black slacks. No shoes. His hair was cut short near the scalp. His eyes were glowing blue and lightning circled his torso, arms, and hands. Gage nodded.

"So, you can control the elements."

"Only lightning."

"Can you make it rain?"

"I have to get out of this cell first."

"Then, you'll agreeing to my offer?"

"Anything for my freedom."

"You have your freedom. Thunderstorm."

"Just use my real name." Thunderstorm said.

"You sure? Because Randy Keith doesn't sound frightful. Thunderstorm works. Because of what you can do."

"Whatever. My real name works enough."

"Understandable."

Randy Keith was set free and left with Hark from Alcatraz. Later in the day, Randy was brought to a secure base to his safety while Gage went out once again to meet with another possible recruit. This time, Hark was sent to Retropolis, to Pegasus Prison. There, he was brought to the cell of a young woman. Wearing brown prison clothes, long black hair with blonde highlights. Make-up covered her face and she was full of energy.

"You're something to look at." Gage said.

"Don't be rude."

"I can be whatever I choose to be."

"Then, there's no equality!"

"Equality is only given to those who fight for it. Plus, it's not for everyone."

"It is for me."

The woman approached the door. A smile on her face, turning back and forth into a frown.

"From what I read in this file, your name is Marian Swanford. But, you prefer to go by Maria Swan instead. Why?"

"Marian Swanford was my birth name. A name for a pleasant housewife or a loving wife. Maria Swan, on the other hand, is a name for a wild card. Someone who isn't afraid to take the risks and dare the truths."

"Where did you get the inspiration to become Maria Swan?"

"Death."

"Death? Like the grim reaper death or like just death?"

"No. Death. You've heard of her, haven't you?"

"Ugh. That Death."

"You've heard of her. Wonderful!"

"Hell, you'll fit right in."

"Right in what?"

"What I've come to offer you."

"You're going to meet with Death?!"

"Something along those lines."

"YES!"

Maria Swan was released by Hark's orders as he took her back the secure base. Thunderstorm was waiting as Maria Swan had entered.

"What exactly is all of this?" He wondered.

As Gage went on to meet the final recruit, he knew Maria's only reason for agreeing was to have a confrontation with Death herself.

IV

ONE SHOT COUNTS

Sitting on a rooftop in the early portion of the night, Blake Smalls sat steady, rifle in hand. Wearing his black and gray militaristic/stealth uniform, he aimed the rifle toward one of the tall buildings in the Downtown section of the city. Through the scope, he sees a man dressed in a nice suit talking with others. Looks to be a corporate party for business-types. Blake prepared the rifle for firing.

"Figured you would be doing something like this." A voice said from behind Blake.

He turned and saw Gage standing by the doorway on the roof. Blake nodded and went back to his business.

"Gage Hark. It's been a while."

"It has."

"As you can see, I am preoccupied at the moment."

"That is true. But, I come with an offer. One you may not want to miss."

"A.B. sent you to find me, didn't she?"

"You know her well enough."

"That is the truth. Figured I would be called back into service eventually. Just not this soon."

"You can thank those rising heroes for that. They're the reason A.B. sent me here to find you. As I have previously done with others."

"I'm not the only one?"

"Not this time. There's a greater concern and it requires a unit to face it."

"What concern?"

"After what happened in Retropolis, things haven't been as natural in the world as the general public would believe."

"Nothing is natural anymore, Gage. Not after the things we've encountered."

"I need to know. Are you coming along?"

Blake aimed the rifle at the businessman. Gage looked on, waiting for a response.

"Give me a moment." Blake said. Paying attention closely.

Blake fired the round, moving across the sky. Breaking through the window and hitting the businessman in the forehead. His body fell to the floor and the entire room turned into a frenzy. Screams of horror and terror merged into one. Blake could see it happening and he grinned.

He arose from his position and approached Gage. Placing the rifle strap over his shoulder.

"I'm with you."

"Good to have you back, Gunbaine."

"Let's get moving. I want to talk with A.B."

V

MEETING OF THE ENFORCEMENT

The following day, Gage arrived at the secure base of A.B., Base 33. Inside, he saw everyone he recruited sitting at a long table. Around the facility were Black Ops soldiers, ready and armed for any precaution. Blake and Randy were the only calm member at the table while Maria Swan was ecstatic, Black Mare felt disgusted at the scenery of a technological place, and Lance Gasper felt disrespected as no one within the base knew who he was.

"So many toys in this place." Maria said.

"Such disgust." Black Mare mentioned.

"Good to see all of you here." Gage said. "Now, take heed as the one who needs you is set to arrive."

"When?" Maria asked.

"When she wants to." A voice said from the entrance.

The recruits turned and saw A.B. approaching the table. Wearing her business attire. She stood at the foot of the table and glanced at everyone.

"There's one missing, Hark."

"Couldn't find him. I left a message for the guy. Not sure if he answered or not."

Roaring sounds began to echo from outside the base. Startling everyone as the soldiers ran toward the entrance. Their arms up and ready to fire. A.B. walked near them as Gage followed her. The recruits remained at the table. The doors had lifted up, revealing a gold and black sports car and in came a man wearing a black and gold racer's suit. Removing his helmet. He looked and saw the soldiers with their guns aimed at him.

"Guess I came at an unexpected time." The racer said. "But, I am here."

"He answered the call." Gage said.

"In his own way." A.B. replied.

A.B. approached the sudden racer and extended her hand toward him. He shook her hand.

"Good you could make it, Mr. Daniel Barns."

"Oh, please. Call me G-Zero, Ms. Brown."

"Noted. Come with me."

A.B., Hark, and G-Zero approached the table as everyone returned to their stations. They all sat at the table, looking at one another. Unsure. Uncertain.

"Listen up." A.B. said. "You are all here for a very important concern."

"How important?" Maria asked.

"I'm aware you're all familiar with the *Battle of Retropolis*. Beings coming down from the sky and causing mayhem. Leading to those rising heroes forming their own unit. Now, they set out to maintain the order in this world.”

“Then, what’s the problem?” Thunderstorm asked.

“The problem is they cannot be the only team operating. Which is why I had Lieutenant Hark recruit each of you. To form a team of my own. One to work in the shadows to get the jobs done.”

“What kind of jobs?” Blake asked.

“You already know the drill, Gunbaine. It’s these others who must learn the rules.”

“Who are we after, Adrian?”

“Death’s operations. They’re still in flux and ongoing.”

“We’re going after Death?!” Maria yelled.

“No. you’re going after her doings. They’re still taking place and The Resistance have yet to uncover her secret plots.”

“What if we run into them while on the mission?”

“Then, you’ll do what must be done or die trying.”

Blake nodded.

“Then I see.”

He glanced around once more at the recruits and stood up.

“So, we’re the Enforcement Order.”

“You can say that.” A.B. said.

“When do we begin?”

“Very soon.”

THE IRE OF FLASHBURN: I AM FLASHBURN

I

<u>CONTACT</u>

After a hard day at the car shop, Floyd Rizzo had finished his task for the day and left. Taking his usual walk home, Floyd is a young man looking to enter the engineering industry. His skill set is known by those in his circle. His clothes were dirty from the work of the day and he couldn't wait to return home for a shower and a drink.

As he walked, he saw a flash of light appear to his right. Stopping as he turned back and saw the light flashing once again. The light resembled a kindling. As if something was set to burn. Floyd decided to have a closer look, since the area was very close to a neighborhood. Floyd approached the light and it vanished, he followed it into a small cavern.

"What is this place?" He wondered.

Inside the cavern, Floyd saw the light once again, yet this time from it arose an ember. A walking ember. Floyd was terrified, yet, intrigued. He didn't run from the walking ember as it approached him and measured him.

"What are you?" He asked.

"I am an elemental." The ember said. "I have lived for eons in existence."

"You have the skill." The ember said. "You can handle the flame."

"I work in engineering. Explains my attraction to the flame."

"But, you're not welder."

"I have some background in that field."

"Then I have chosen wisely."

"I'm just curious. Even though I'm not freaking out while talking to a living, walking fire. Do you have a name?"

"My name is The Incandescence."

"That sounds… interesting."

The ember touched Floyd with its finger. Through Floyd's body flowed a living fire that could be seen flowing underneath his skin.

"What is happening to me?!" Floyd yelled.

"I have given you a portion of my power."

Floyd's eyes set themselves on fire as he yelled. Feeling the burning effect. After a few seconds, Floyd had fell to the ground and the ember stood over him.

"You will awaken, and you will become a new creature. A creature with the powers of the element of fire. You will become *Flashburn*."

Hours later during the night, Floyd awoke from inside the cavern, seeing no sign of the walking ember or the kindling light of fire. Heading out of the cave, he sees its nightfall and he ran home. Unsure of what happened to him. As he ran, small combustions of fire started to form from his hands. Kindling across his fingers. He looked at them and patted them on his pants. Putting the fire out.

"What is this? What am I feeling inside of me?" He asked himself.

II

<u>WHAT HAVE I BECOME?</u>

Floyd returned home and ran to the bathroom. Staring at himself through the mirror, he could glance fire within his eyes and see it moving through his hands and arms. Unsure of what was taking place within him, he could only wonder for a moment and after several seconds the fire ceased and silenced. Floyd could no longer feel the urging burn from within.

"It stopped. Finally."

Floyd chose to sleep off the remaining effects of the kindling for the night. The following day, he went to a laboratory he's known for helping in his spare time. Walking through the lab doors, he is greeted by Professor Dan Simon.

"Good to see you again, Mr. Rizzo."

"I'm here for a dire need."

"How dire are you talking?"

"It's difficult to explain."

"I see." Simon replied. "Come with me to my office. You can tell me all about it there."

They walked into his office. Simon had shut the door and

Floyd sat down. Simon walked over to his desk and faced the young man.

"What is it?"

"I don't know how to put it."

"Whatever it is, you can tell me."

Floyd nodded nervously.

"On my way home yesterday, I came across a cave."

"A cave?"

"Yeah. Didn't know it was there before. But, it was."

"And what drove you to find this cave?"

"A light. Looked like fire."

"What did you find inside the cave?"

"A living fire. It walked and spoke. Just like I'm speaking to you."

"Like the burning bush?"

"Not in that detail."

"I see." Simon has said. "What did this living fire say?"

"That I was a chosen vessel. To bring forth its purpose. To become Flashburn."

"Flashburn? Like that old fable?"

"Yeah."

"Yet, that would mean the living fire was the Incandescence. The mythological elemental entity of fire."

"He's no myth. He exists. He placed something within me. A burning fire. Kindling from time to time."

"The Incandescence has chosen you to be its vessel. He called you Flashburn."

"He did. What is all of this? I'm not familiar with the whole scenario of its history."

"Lucky for you, I am."

Simon stood up from his desk and went to the door. Floyd watched him as he prepared to open the door.

"Professor?"

"Meet me at my home later this evening. I will explain everything there."

"How much do you know about this?"

"I have a friend who delves into myths and legends. I will speak to him and give you all he tells me. But, for right now, return home or to your work. Get your mind off the Incandescence and this Flashburn."

"Yes sir."

III

<u>WHAT BURNS MORE THAN FIRE?</u>

Floyd went to Professor Simon's home later in the evening. There, the two discussed the Incandescence and what it was capable of. Floyd could feel the heat surging within his being. It was slowly rising throughout the coming hours.

"It's of ancient origin." Simon told Floyd.

"How ancient?"

"I do not know. But, whatever it has granted you, is the same as times past."

"There were others that have gone through this?"

"Precisely. How many? I do not know. But this is no coincidence."

"Then, what is a Flashburn?"

"A Flashburn is someone who inherits the power of the Incandescence. Which is you in this era. You said the Incandescence touched you and you felt its fire purging within you."

"Yes. I can feel it now. Kindling within my body. Through my chest, my arms, and my hands."

"You're bind to him. To his power."

"Until?"

"Until you either die or your purpose is complete."

"That's good to hear." Floyd said sarcastically.

"This might serve some good, Floyd. With the rising heroes across the world, maybe you can join in their ranks."

"I have no interest of being some kind of superhero."

"Not a superhero. A protector of the world. From the threats foreign and domestic."

"Sounds like some Nathan Hawke speech."

"Good thing I'm not him."

"There's that."

The TV in the room blinked on and showing the local news. Downtown has been visited by a man, whose hands are glowing with red-orange flames. He walked throughout the streets, scorching whatever was in his sights. He saw he news camera and ran toward it. Snatching the camera, revealing his face for all to see. A young man with scruffy brown hair.

"Since everyone is becoming a hero, I have chosen to be an adversary. An atomic bomb to the world!"

"You want to test out your powers?"

"Not sure if I could."

The kindling within him grew stronger to the point of flames combusting from his hands. His eyes glowed as bright as a fire. Simon watched as Floyd was being transformed.

"This is why he chose you." Simon said.

Floyd ran out of the home and within seconds he bolted into the air as Simon saw. Fire trailing behind him through the night sky.

245

IV

<u>I AM FLASHBURN</u>

The man calling himself the Atomic Bomb continued decimating all that was in his sights throughout the town. Civilians ran in fear of the raging flames streaming across the roads. Buildings burning from the first floor as Atomic Bomb walked through the streets.

"I will show you all how dangerous one man truly is."

A roaring sound came from above. Atomic had gazed up and saw a flying fire coming toward him. He moved out of the road as the fire crashed. From the rubble arose Floyd, yet, he wasn't the same. He wasn't wearing his causal clothing. His shirt was gone. His jeans had vanished. Instead, he was dressed in a uniform with the colors of red and orange. Fire emitted continually from his head, hands, and body. His eyes were the color of a raging flame.

"Who are you supposed to be?"

"An ire yet to burn!"

Flashburn rushed and delivered punches to Atomic Bomb. He bounced back, rubbing his face with a grin.

"Physical feats won't stop me! I have the power to nuke this place and that is my will!"

Atomic raised his hand, preparing to transform himself into a nuclear bomb. Flashburn thought for a mere second and within his being, the Incandescence spoke to him. A clear voice with a sincere purpose. Flashburn nodded.

"I know what to do."

Flashburn stretched forth his arms and from them emitted an vapor of fire, which surrounded Atomic Bomb and sucked the nuclear power from his body, leaving him to fall on the pavement, unconscious. Flashburn took Atomic's power and made it his own. Simon had reached the town and witnessed the event. Flashburn turned, seeing him. He nodded and flew off into the air.

The following day, Simon paid a visit to Floyd's home, where he found him working on a car in the garage. Floyd seemed like his usual self. Nothing major had changed.

"I just came to pay a visit. To see how you were doing."

"I'm doing well, Professor. Nothing gone wrong yet."

"That's good to hear. I have to ask. Do you remember anything from last night?"

Floyd put down the tools and stood up from the car, wiping his dirty hands with the nearby towel.

"Truthfully, I do."

"Everything?"

"Everything. And it's just to start."

"You're going to go along with the Incandescence's will?"

"I have no other choice, Professor. I am Flashburn."

Somewhere else, a young man sat outside, overlooking a lake. From behind him came a whisper. He turned, no one was there. Going back to his business, he was confronted by a being that appeared to be made of darkness. The being uttered something in the young man's ear and placed its hand on his forehead. The young man twitched as the dark figure vanished. The young man stood up and walked away from the lake and as he did, his body transformed into a living shadow. Dark as the night sky, yet in the day.

ABOUT THE AUTHOR

Ty'Ron W. C. Robinson II is the author of several works of fiction. Including the *Dark Titan Universe Saga* series (*Dark Titan Knights, The Resistance Protocol, Tales of the Scattered, Tales of the Numinous, Day of Octagon*) and *The Haunted City Saga* series. Also of other books (*Lost in Shadows, Hod, The Book of The Elect, Symbolum Venatores, etc.*) and One-Shot short stories More information pertaining to the author and stories can be found at darktitanentertainment.com.